Created with Vellum

Land Glorious

*A Thrilling Tale of Mortals Lost in Faerie,
Unruly Alchemists, Philtrecraft Unfiltered,
the Miraculous Construction of a Bloodthirsty
House of Flowers and Sorrowful Secrets
Sensationally Spilled...*

Tansy Rayner Roberts

Contents

Ygraine

granddaughter of Charlotte, daughter of Isolda, sister of Iseult

Orlando Device came to my window, the night before my wedding. I heard a tap-tap-tap on my window and looked up to see a clockwork robin, shiny with brass polish, gazing in at me with an expression one could only describe as plaintive.

I opened the window, taking satisfaction in the plinking sound as the glass hit the robin, and the robin hit the courtyard stone, two floors below us.

"Harsh," said the man on the balcony.

I stared at him, not knowing what he could possibly have to say to me. It didn't matter. He couldn't break my heart again. "What do you want, Orlando?"

If you've never met Orlando Device, let me save you some time: he's the most beautiful creature that ever walked the earth, if your type is chaotic Chinese gentlemen with deep, soulful eyes, wild black hair, and grease smears on his cuffs. He doesn't look real. He looks like he has stepped out of a book of fairy tales, and he's here to eat your soul.

The worst of it is, he always looked like that: before and after.

I glanced up and down the balcony, which ran along the length of the side of the building, connecting many family rooms together. No Rinaldo in sight. "Where's your keeper?"

Everyone else thinks Rinaldo is the sensible brother, the one who keeps Orlando in check. I used to think that, too, before I discovered what the sensible brother was capable of.

"Rinaldo said I should leave you alone," said Orlando, looking mournful.

"I assume you're not planning to ask me to elope with you." This was one of those bleak jokes that only one person in the conversation understands.

He gazed at me like a puppy well aware that it's about to be kicked. "Ygraine. Are you really going to do this?"

"Am I going to marry the man chosen for me when I was seventeen, and become the Duchess of Cornwall and Land's End? Yes."

Princesses don't get much of a say in these things, me least of all: the youngest of six. At least I wouldn't be sent out of the country, like Iseult and Evanna and Unity.

Orlando's expression darkened, which did not render him any less of an illustration of wayward handsomeness, right out of *Girl's Own Journal*. "Ygraine. Are you seriously going to take the love philtre tomorrow?"

～

It was a loaded question, given my family history. Love philtres haven't done the House of Camlough-Pendragon any favours.

My grandmother, Queen Charlotte, was born during the Regency: an era of wild parties, disruptive royal scandals, and a fervent fashion for love philtres. Everyone knew that her own father, then the Prince Regent, did not love his wife. He treated Princess Caroline abominably, casting her aside as soon as he impregnated her.

Charlotte's wedding to Cormac Camlough, cousin to the King of Eire, is recorded in history books as the first time that man and wife chose to take the love philtre as part of a Britannian marriage ceremony; it was to spite her father, I suppose, but it did rather create a rod for everyone else's back.

On the day of his coronation, the new King George had Princess Caroline barred from London so she could never share his reign. She died soon after.

Charlotte, the king's only heir, was so furious at this behaviour that she and her husband upped sticks and left Britannia for Eire. Her daughter Isolda was born in exile: quite against convention for a future queen of Britannia to give birth to the next queen in another kingdom.

When she returned to rule, Queen Charlotte's reign was stable, and lacking her father's drama. She ruled for eleven years, and while there was criticism among the populace for her court looking 'a little too Eirish for their tastes, there was little for them to criticise.

Queen Charlotte died when her daughter Isolda was twenty (the same age I am now), and the new queen chose her own husband.

Queen Isolda met Percival Pendragon, a poor Welsh nobleman, at a ball with the theme 'Tournament of Roses'. Both were masked when they fell in love, which is about as much romance as any royal can expect in this day and age. She married him, despite the protests from all sides.

They had six daughters. Iseult, Evanna, Oonagh, Arwenna, Unity and Ygraine. Isolda chose Eirish names for most of my sisters, in defiance of the whispers that had followed her around since her birth: that being born in another country made her less of a queen, somehow.

A favourite phrase of hers I remember from childhood: "Defeating fools is best done with pageantry."

Isolda celebrated Eirish artists and poets in her early court just as, later, she brought her Indian favourites into the palace, and representatives of other colonies. As if anyone was likely to forget she had conquered the world.

In Isolda's final triumph over the court of public opinion, she betrothed her eldest daughter, Iseult, to Marcas, the King of Eire (a second cousin something removed). That was when it all started to go wrong.

~

Iseult was born fourteen years before me; at five years old, I barely knew her when she left us. I remember her wedding only because it had the honey cakes I liked, and someone played the harp too loudly. I was dressed as a fairy in a green dress with wings. All six of us wore matching dresses, and famous gentlemen took photographs of us in a meadow.

Page boys were dressed as goblins carrying marzipan fruits, like something out of Christina Rossetti's popular poem: the one that that had every girl in London daydreaming of being stolen away while picking blackberries in the country.

I remember crying because I bit into a peach and got a mouthful of almond paste. I suppose I was an ungrateful child, but I had been looking forward to that peach.

At some point, two love philtres were 'accidentally' dropped: one into Iseult's cup and the other into the cup of Tristan Lyonesse, a handsome young nephew of the king and heir to the Duchies of Cornwall and Land's End.

Love philtres are overwhelming enough when you know you've been dosed. According to her friends, Iseult believed she had genuinely fallen in love with the wrong person at the worst possible time: her husband's nephew, on her wedding day.

Three years later, Iseult was dead at the hands of King Mark, as was her young lover, in a tragedy so brutal that no one was even willing to write poems about it. A lady-in-waiting later confessed to the authorities that she had administered the philtre to Iseult at the behest of Tristan himself...

The war that followed was brief and brutal, and when it was done, there were no more kings and queens of Eire.

(It feels day by day as if every country in the world belongs to Britannia. My mother has eaten them all.)

Iseult was the first of my sisters to die because of a love philtre. She was not the last.

"Yes," I told Orlando, the night before my wedding. "Of course I'm going to take the love philtre."

My preferred option of *no husband at all, if you please* was no option at all, not for the daughter of the Empress of Britannia.

A love philtre might make my life bearable. I

wouldn't let it rule me or wreck me, as it had my sisters. I was stronger than them.

This way, it was my choice.

"Ygraine," Orlando begged, his messy black hair falling in his eyes as he leaned against the railing. The metal staves of the ironwork leaned towards him, like a flower leaning into the sun. "We can get you out of this. We'll think of something."

"Don't you dare," I commanded. "Orlando Device. If you or your brother do anything to ruin my wedding, I will hate you forever."

I went indoors, put myself to bed, and dreamed of golden cups filled with philtres that would change my life.

Better drowned than duffers, if not duffers won't drown.

— Arthur Ransome, *Swallows and Amazons*, 1930

Chapter 1

In Which Orlando Faces A Fury, and Rinaldo Does Not Drown

The fogswept gardens of Buckingham Palace were beautiful at night. Flavia had not realised what a difference it would make, to stand on lawn that sprawled out in all directions rather than the tiny postage stamp gardens available to most London residents.

The trees were delighted to have a faerie standing among them; even the tree currently housing the disreputable if miraculous Mr Orlando Device was emitting a general warmth in Flavia's direction.

She would feel completely welcome here, under the chilly sky and the dim, greenish moonlight (the moon was trying its hardest, but the damp fog blanketing the city was winning the battle) if it were not for the furious princess standing before them.

Ygraine Victoria Camlough Pendragon, Duchess of Cornwall and Land's End, Viscountess Lyon, the youngest daughter of the Empress of Britannia, was a commanding young lady. She wore a heavy, swooping hooded cloak of embroidered silk which was clearly intended to be worn over a much larger dress; it shrouded her in midnight blue, which was almost as good as black for sneaking around.

Her dark eyes blazed with fury at Orlando; she barely seemed to notice Flavia's existence.

Orlando himself, leaning out of the branches of a tree, should be at least slightly unsettled by this alarming situation — they had been caught red-handed in the palace gardens, by a member of the Royal family. The only thing worse (as far as Flavia was concerned) was if the person who had caught them was a butler.

Instead, Orlando looked strangely delighted. "Stay right there!" he exclaimed, disentangling himself from the branches.

Princess Ygraine and Flavia made identical scoffing noises, then glanced quickly at each other in a shared moment of understanding. Clearly, the Device brothers created frustration wherever they went.

"Miss Wednesday," Flavia introduced herself. "I'm a governess."

"Well," said Princess Ygraine with a twist of her mouth. "It's good to know someone responsible has been watching him. We should have hired a governess years ago."

Orlando managed to dash himself out of the tree with the same level of headstrong fervour with which he climbed up in the first place. He had removed a small cloth bundle from this hiding place and now attempted to hide his bounty inside his coat.

The princess was too quick for him; she leaped forward with her lantern swinging and seized his wrist.

Orlando froze, clearly not willing to be rough with her. Princess Ygraine had no such restraint.

"What have you there?" she demanded, shaking him. "Are you a thief as well as everything else?"

A look of regret passed over Orlando's face. "I've seen the wanted posters, highness. I know what 'everything else' you think of me."

"So you should," she fumed. Even in the unflattering light of the lantern, surrounded on all sides by greenish fog, even with her face twisted with anger, Princess Ygraine was really quite lovely.

Flavia had only seen her face before in royal portraits, usually in mourning dress alongside an ever-dwindling number of sisters, and sometimes in the fashion sketches, though there had been little need to consult those since she left Dorchester Grove, her place of employment before she joined the Gloucester family. Queenie Gloucester was a little too young to care about what the fashionable young ladies were wearing to balls.

"I put something here for safekeeping," Orlando said in a low voice. "It has nothing to do with you. There was no need to set traps."

"You went away," the princess said, her tone quite

vicious. "You two *complete disasters* blew up my life, sabotaged my wedding, and abandoned me to my mother. More to the point, you *took my husband with you*."

"Orlando," said Flavia, quite shocked. "Did you and Rinaldo abduct the Duke of Cornwall?" She had known they were on the run due to some royal crime, but this was a shade beyond the pale. "Where on earth have you been keeping him?"

Orlando let out a heavy sigh, as if having to explain his antics was the worst thing that had happened to him all week. A bit rich, considering that he had recently lost his brother, half the Gloucester family and a yellow cat in an explosion that had sent them all to the Isle of Faerie.

Princess Ygraine folded her arms, staring him directly in the eye despite being many inches shorter; Flavia saw the resemblance now to the intimidating Queen Isolda whose portrait glared out from every wall, every coin and every postage stamp. "Yes, Orlando. Where have you been hiding my husband?"

Orlando laid a gentle hand over the top of her fingers, where Ygraine was still holding his cuff. "Can we go somewhere quieter to discuss this? And warmer. Miss Wednesday is chilled to the bone."

True, but Flavia was used to ignoring her own physical distress. "Don't bring me into this. Tell the poor woman where you've stashed her missing husband."

Ygraine startled as if she was not accustomed to being thought of as a 'poor woman.' Flavia had never taken the time to learn etiquette around royalty. Apparently, random bursts of pity were not appropriate.

"I'm waiting," the princess said, her anger still simmering in her posture, her voice and those dark, furious eyes of hers. Fury suited her. Flavia rather admired it. She could not remember the last time she had properly allowed herself to get angry about anything — she always had to be so careful, so controlled.

Orlando's face was pained. "Until recently, he's had the run of Lady Mortmain's townhouse in Actaeon Place," he admitted. "You met him, Miss Wednesday. He was of some assistance in rescuing us from the cellars — which goes to show Cornwall, at least, doesn't hold a grudge," he added in a defiant tone. "Though I can't say his personality has improved. He was much more amiable as a human."

Flavia frowned. He couldn't mean... "Orlando," she breathed. "Did you turn the Duke of Cornwall and Land's End into a yellow clockwork cat?"

R inaldo Device dreamed of bronze. Under his hands, the house took shape: its rooms and ceilings, floors and staircases. He kneaded the warm metal into windows and chairs and tables; with the edge of his thumbnail he carved floral wallpaper, portraits for the walls, and a detailed series of bells and pulleys culminating in the butler's pantry.

He shaped a perfect bronze bathtub and set it in place just as water burst out of the taps. The water filled the bath and spilled over, running down the staircases, pouring from room to room.

It was an elaborate dance, the water and the bronze: not a house after all, but a fountain that gathered and poured and tipped, all in a perfect sequence.

Rinaldo swam from room to room. He did not need to breathe; the bronze protected him. The water warmed him.

All was as it should be.

Light gleamed above him. The attics. He had to remember something about the attics...

But, no. That didn't matter. Better to float here, surrounded by his bronze walls, safe and sound.

Pain burst through the top of Rinaldo's head as something — someone — grabbed his hair. Up, then. No choice but up. He kicked and swam and burst, somehow, into fresh air that tasted impossibly of summer sunshine.

A girl with a serious face loomed over him, her

hands wound tightly in his hair. It took him a dazed moment or two to recognise Little Miss Queenie Gloucester, whom he had last seen exhausted and miserable in an attic, in the middle of the night. It was not night now.

"Idiot," said Miss Gloucester, summoning enough scorn that it was astounding her flannel night-rail did not catch fire. "Are all grownups this stupid?"

Rinaldo crawled to the bank and lay there for a moment, wheezing for breath. His chest hurt with every ragged gasp. "It doesn't come by accident," he rasped. "We have to take a special class in stupid when we turn seventeen."

They were not in Actaeon Place anymore. It was warm, and the air had a sort of stickiness to it. Were they even in Britannia? Rinaldo had his doubts.

Glossy green willow branches 'wept' all along the river, but there were other trees too that he barely recognised, some sporting enormous flowers in a bright array of colours. "Is this the Forest of Arden?" he wondered aloud. If so, it had perked up since their first visit. This forest felt alive and fresh rather than pale and stagnant.

"If we're lucky," said Miss Gloucester. "I can think of worse places we could be." She hugged her knees, looking miserable. Her slippers were grubby, and her hem torn.

Rinaldo could think of a few worse places himself. This was a green and pleasant land, all right, but the lack of winter was a concern. How far had they travelled, to leave the season behind? "Any sign of the others? Who else came through with us?"

It was all such a muddle in his head. The fountain had broken, he remembered that... no, he had broken the fountain. Destroyed his own work, to thwart Lady Mortmain's plot. But it had all gone wrong. He remembered steam and shouting, the feeling that he had been punched in the head from the inside out...

And then, nothing. Nothing but drowning. Thank goodness for Miss Gloucester.

"I've seen no one," the girl said quietly. "Dash was right by my side when it all happened, but I can't find him. I've been walking for hours — at least, it felt like hours. You're the first person I saw, and you were..." She gave him a look that was rather sharp under the circumstances. "You're lucky I spotted you. What on earth were you doing in that river?"

"Drowning," said Rinaldo. "It made some sort of sense at the time."

He couldn't have been underwater since they arrived, could he? Not if Miss Gloucester had been walking for hours.

"There are some hills over there," the girl said, pointing beyond the lush bright trees. "I thought perhaps we could climb to the top of one and get a better idea of our surroundings. And when I say we, I mean you, because I'm in my night things and my feet hurt."

Rinaldo nodded. "Good plan. If my brother is anywhere nearby, chances are he'll have set fire to something by now. We'll spot the plume of smoke." He gave her feet a concerned look. She had slippers, at least. It wasn't like she had been roaming the forests barefoot. "Do you really want to wait here while I go for help?"

"I suppose not," sighed Miss Gloucester. "It's most inconvenient, being valiant," she added.

"Tell me about it." Rinaldo squelched as he walked, though he could feel that his clothes were already starting to dry off in this thick warm air.

They reached the nearest hill and headed up the slope; there was little breath left to make conversation.

Rinaldo worried about Orlando. He often worried about Orlando, but usually it was with the luxury of having him nearby, so that he could witness all of his terrible life choices at first hand. It wasn't that Orlando was stupid, except about women, but he trailed disaster behind him like the fluttering tail of a kite.

Rinaldo was not quite as sensible and earnest as he had been as a child — he had reluctantly embraced the chaos that came from being one of the Miraculous and Extraordinary Device Brothers. Certainly, he was far less cautious now: Orlando's bold attitude to life had contaminated him thoroughly. Rinaldo lived more adventurously than he ever would have done without the boy who entered his life when he was eight years old and taught him to build toy trains out of stolen spoons and hairpins.

Separated from Orlando, he felt like he was missing an arm.

"This is an island," said Miss Gloucester, breaking into Rinaldo's thoughts of the time before he had a brother. "Look."

They had reached the crest of the hill, and a rocky outcrop with a steep cliff falling away below them. The warmth of the weather was more intense here, away from the dark and leafy trees. It felt thick and strange, with such a powerful scent of flowers that the atmosphere was almost drugging. Rinaldo gazed where the girl pointed, and he could indeed see the curve of the land and the bright blue water beyond. It looked like the kind of island one might find in a story-book about pirates. "I have a bad feeling about this," he said.

"I want to go home," Miss Gloucester sighed, and sat down on the soft grass with a fwump. "This isn't Britannia, is it? I can't imagine there's anywhere in Britannia as hot as this."

"Within the Britannian Empire, perhaps," said Rinaldo, thinking of what he had learned of all the colonies in recent years. "But, no. This is not Britannia." A cloud of butterflies swished past his face, and he startled, all but teetering backwards over the cliff.

"Mr Device!" Miss Gloucester cried, catching at his hand so he fell forward rather than back. He landed on the grass beside her, at least, not crushing the girl herself.

"What —" he started to say, and then another winged thing swooped over his head, laughed maniacally at them both in a chattering voice, and buzzed away. "That wasn't a butterfly," he said in a voice of deadly calm.

"No," squeaked Miss Gloucester.

"It was a fairy."

"Yes, it was a fairy." They both sat in silence for a moment. "I'm not going to call you Mr Device any more," she said. "It's too long to shout out if you're in trouble."

"Seems reasonable," Rinaldo agreed. "Can I call you Queenie or do you prefer Miss Gloucester?"

"Queenie is fine unless my mother is nearby. Then it has to be Petronella."

"My condolences."

They sat in silence a little while longer, taking it all in.

"Faerie, then," she said in a business-like voice. "That's where we are. The Isle of Faerie. My goodness. I should have read those storybooks my governess kept stealing for Dash. Do you think Miss Wednesday will rescue us?"

Rinaldo looked around at the wild green majesty of the island below them. He had always wanted to travel, but this was so far beyond the exotic lands he had dreamed of reaching. "We can only hope," he said finally. "I don't feel a great presence of metal around here, which limits my magic greatly."

"We're also lacking an alchemical lab," Queenie sighed. "That sinks me. What should our first action be?"

Rinaldo stood up, straightening his trousers. They had survived the near-drowning and the hike. They'd have to survive a little longer. He wasn't sure how to answer her — with something inspiring and vague, no doubt. But then he saw a familiar and annoying yellow shape flash in and out of the trees below them, so what he said was: "We need to follow that cat. He must have come through with us. He was in the attic before."

"You want to chase a cat around the forests of Faerie?" Queenie protested. "Why on earth should we?"

"For the sake of my honour," Rinaldo said grimly. "For a friend I let down badly. Also, it might the only thing made out of metal on this entire island."

"See," said Queenie, standing up and brushing the grass from her long, pale nightdress. "That last argument holds water. Next time, start with the practical and work your way up to honour and sentiment."

Ygraine

and Uncle Albert's Orphans

The Device Brothers were Uncle Albert's fault.

For as long as I could remember, Uncle Albert (really a cousin by marriage, but it was easier for everyone to be uncles) and my father Percival shared a mutual obsession with improving Buckingham Palace. My earliest memory of Papa was of him dismantling a dumbwaiter, so it could be mechanised.

I was three years old, and I remember the scent of his tobacco as Papa lifted me in his arms and placed me entirely inside the dumbwaiter, then pressed the button to send me hurtling down to the kitchens.

I screamed all the way down.

We had a darling cook who always had a sugar pig or a biscuit for little princesses. It was she who seized a pale and terrified child out of the little lift, hugging me and cosseting me until I could be calm again.

When Papa burst into the kitchens, having taken the steps two at a time, he bellowed, "Did it work?"

~

I was not allowed to sit at the front in the abbey during my father's funeral, though I was nearly eight and quite ladylike enough to behave myself. I was squashed between Cousin Victoria (always *cousin* Victoria, she refused to aunt) and Uncle Albert in the third row, well apart from the grieving queen and my elder, more presentable sisters.

Three hymns into the service, I discovered that dear Uncle Albert had filled his left pocket with comfits, so I might dip my hand in and out.

At the end of the grim affair, just as I thought I might vomit liquorice-flavoured sugar all over the shining abbey floor tiles, Uncle Albert leaned in and whispered to me in his thick Germanian accent. "I have had an idea about moving stairs."

"Don't bother the child," hissed Cousin Victoria.

Papa would have loved moving stairs. I gave Uncle Albert a tiny nod and he replied with a wink.

~

The years of deep mourning are best skipped over. Mama's misery soaked into the walls of Buckingham

Palace, weighing us all down and making us feel guilty at snatching any moment of fresh air and happiness. Grief wore on thanks to that awful business with Iseult and Prince Tristan, then Oonagh's death less than a year after her own wedding.

Mama returned to herself after that, but not for us. Even her obsession with stamping out the fairy fashions of the day was a sideline to her true work. When Queen Isolda lifted her head out of mourning and returned to the world, it was as the Iron Widow, Empress of Britannia. Imperial business became her meat and drink, and her thoughts never quite returned to the domestic details of palace life.

Uncle Albert took this disinterest as permission to carry on with his own work however he liked. Such as the introduction of the moving staircase, which hiccuped and belched steam if anyone heavier than a small child stepped upon it. (Guess who was the small child?)

Steam automation invaded every corner of the palace, but the workshop in particular. My sisters and cousins refused to go near it, citing the smell of iron or the unpleasant heat of the steam that rolled off the various half-built engines.

It was my refuge, away from the pinching fingers of my sisters and the dread of yet another wedding to plan (Arwenna this time, betrothed to the Marquess of Dorset). Albert's workshop was warm and comforting, a source of candied fruits and busywork suited to my small hands.

Cousin Victoria tolerated her husband's interest in palace improvements, though in public she complimented his excellent taste in art and furnishings rather than the mechanics behind them. Thanks to Mama's disinterest, the renovations of the palace could easily have fallen to Victoria herself — but with Albert so enthusiastic, she was able to devote her days to her own work: charities, luncheons, and the arranging of political marriages for her many sons and daughters. Cousin Victoria's children have been carefully decanted into European countries where there is no fashion for love philtres. She had learned from Queen Isolda's experiences.

Over dinner one night, and then another night, and then a third night, Uncle Albert made mention of two orphan boys whose magical talents had caught his eye. "Metallurmagery, that's the way of the future," he declared. "No one can be expected to run a clockwork palace without that extra spark. Imagine a kitchen where the pots and pans come where they are called! A miniature train to carry elderly relatives from room to room!"

My grandfather Cormac Camlough, former Prince Regent, now an elderly grump with no official role at court, slurped his soup vengefully.

Uncle Albert would not be swayed. He kept talking about these boys, thinking out loud how useful it would be to have them working alongside him.

"Somewhat exploitative, my dear?" Victoria murmured in the calm tone she reserved for disagreeing with her beloved husband.

"How many lads under ten years of age work in the palace kitchens, *nein*?" Albert demanded. "I saw five of them in there the other day turning chickens on spits like something from Henry the Eight's day!"

Mama, her mind on conquest and paperwork, ignored the whole matter.

"What were you doing in the kitchens, Uncle Albert?" I asked over apple pudding one night.

"Why, measuring for heating pipes in the floor, of course," he said, pleased by my interest. "I want our cooks to have the warmest feet in Britannia! Those boys will be able to help me. Do you not agree, Isolda?"

"I suppose so," Mama said absently.

Albert's genius was not limited to inventions; he also had a knack for getting his own way.

A few mornings later, I retreated to the workshop after hearing Arwenna's latest wedding idea (she wanted her pug dog as maid of honour and was after me to carry the thing on a cushion).

Instead of Uncle Albert, I came face to face with an earnest-looking brown boy a little taller than me.

"Hello," I said. He had kind eyes, and dark eyebrows. I had never seen such dark eyebrows, not even on the servants of the envoys of the Raj, who always wore a most splendid array of turbans.

"Hello," the boy said back. "I'm Richard."

"Rinaldo!" yelled a voice from across the workshop.

"Sorry, yes. I'm Rinaldo."

"Don't you know your own name?" I asked, swishing past him to take up my usual space on the bench. I liked to sit up there, for the best view of Uncle Albert's projects. He grumbled in Germanian if I got underfoot.

My uncle was nowhere in sight, and neither was the owner of that rather rude voice, though a pair of bright new boots wiggled from beneath a bronze statue of Pan from the courtyard fountain.

"We changed them," Rinaldo said, watching me as I settled among the wrenches. "These names fit better. We're Rinaldo and Orlando Device."

"If you want to go around falling in love with the wrong people, being trapped by evil enchantresses, and running mad through magical forests, I suppose they're just the thing," I observed. I had spent a great deal of my childhood reading up on chivalric romances, which I found a little more exciting than tales about fairies and goblins, mostly because there were more swords involved.

Rinaldo looked twitchy. "Can I help you with something?"

I felt a stab of anger. I wasn't a *visitor*. "I'm here to inspect you," I said loftily. "On behalf of Queen Isolda."

The other boy slid out from beneath the statue and stared at me with challenge in his eyes. His features reminded me of the son of the Chinese envoy, who had worn blue silk and glared at me during an entire diplomatic banquet. "I don't believe you," said the boy called Orlando. "You're just a girl."

"A princess," I corrected.

He actually laughed at me. "That's worse!"

Rinaldo looked horrified. "We're not used to princesses," he burst out. "Ought we to bow?"

"As if you know how," mocked Orlando.

I racked my brain for something proper to say to them — something appropriate and royal. When I opened my mouth, what came out was: "You're not brothers. You made that up."

The Indian boy looked dejected, as if it were no more than he expected. The Chinese boy squared his shoulders and faced me down. "Say that again and I'll fight you."

"I'm a princess," I reminded him again.

Orlando shrugged, undaunted. "I'll fight you, *your highness*."

"You'll be hearing from the Queen," I said archly, and left the workshop with the maximum of flounce.

After that, I left those boys alone. I enjoyed the look of apprehension and worry that crossed their faces when we passed each other in the corridors, and I shot them sinister looks when no one else was looking.

It's never too early to train young men that a princess is something to be feared.

By 1878, Isolda Camlough Pendragon held the Empire of Britannia, now including England or "Small Anglia," Scotia, Cymru and Eire as well as Canada, the Netherlands, Nova Holland, Van Diemen's Land, Nova Zeeland, Hong Kong, Egypt, Nigeria, and most recently of all: India. European countries paying tribute to Britannia as vassal-states included Frankia, Germania, Belgium and Luxembourg.

The armies of Britannia, armed as they were with superior equipment and technology, including automata and magically armoured vehicles developed in secret over decades, rolled over all who would stand in the way of the Empress.

At the beginning of December 1878, an ultimatum had been issued from the office of the Empress of Britannia to the King of Zululand, in the expectation of her next war. Plans were being drawn for a Britannian invasion into the Boer territories of the Transvaal Republic.

*South Africa was not the only land in the
sights of this conquering queen: documents
were later found explicitly confirming that
Isolda's Ministry of Conquest had been
building a plan to re-take the Americas by force.*

*Were it not for the Siege of Buckingham
Palace and the extraordinary events that
followed in winter 1878, the map of the world
might look very different today.*

— Prof. Eamonn Bendigo, *Isoldan
Britannia: A Deconstruction*, 1956.

Chapter 2

In Which Our Travellers Escape The Winter Chill

Flavia and Orlando followed the cranky princess down a pathway through empty winter trees, along the edge of the ornamental lake. She looked like a wraith in her deep hooded cloak of midnight blue silk.

Flavia jolted as the chilly air around her changed quite suddenly to warm and humid, wondering if the princess had somehow activated an unknown gateway into the Forest of Arden. But no; they were still within the grounds of Buckingham Palace.

And the trees were *green*.

This was all taking too long. Queenie and Dash were in Faerie, at the mercy of Flavia's mother. Time did not always travel the same in Faerie as it did in their world — you could not rely that someone you left there would look the same when you saw them next.

Faeries might not age, but the Gloucester children were mortal. Vulnerable.

She stared impatiently at Orlando's coat, where he had hidden the bundle of philtres. They did not have time to placate princesses.

"It's a combination of pipes and sparks that creates the artificial warmth," Ygraine said indifferently, as the three of them walked through a small orchard of flowering trees that should not be flowering in this country, let alone at this time of year. (The trees gave off waves of smugness about the whole endeavour.)

"One of Rinaldo's pet projects," said Orlando, explaining for Flavia's sake. "At least we won't freeze to death while we're raked over the coals."

The princess gave him a vicious look over her shoulder, and marched along to a stone pavilion with coloured glass windows. There were benches placed along the outside of it, though Flavia would have been just as happy to curl up on the scented grasses if they must sit.

Sitting, apparently, was required for ladies. Flavia and Ygraine perched on a warm stone bench while Orlando hovered over them, clearly on the verge of bursting out with some confession. It was the most awkward tea party ever, made worse by the absence of tea.

"So," said Princess Ygraine in a crisp voice. "Shall we discuss the ruination of my wedding?"

"The mechanical bridesmaids were not our fault,"

Orlando said firmly. "We told her Majesty that automata can be funny about perfumes, but she ordered in a hundredweight of yellow roses and orange blossom. No wonder they started dancing so erratically..."

The princess gave him an impatient look. "Do you think I'm cross because of a few Parisian whirls?"

The exhaustion was beginning to creep up on Flavia. She was light-headed from being surrounded by garden after avoiding trees and plants for most of her London visit. Here in this strange tropical grotto, she was a starving woman with a banquet laid before her. Her green arm, the one woven from daisies and clover, twitched to explore the enormous parks she could feel behind her.

Then, there was that other longing. Orlando had the Water of Worlds in his pocket. They could go to Faerie *now*.

"I still can't believe you did such a thing to Archie," Ygraine continued angrily. "Out of pique, I suppose."

"It was an accident!" Orlando insisted. "It's true we wanted to create a distraction, but..."

The princess laughed hollowly. "Nothing like transforming the bridegroom into a *mechanical cat* to take all eyes off the bride."

"It wasn't in the plan!" Orlando exclaimed. "And I might add, the transformation revealed all manner of ungentlemanly traits in your husband, Ygraine. Cornwall is the worst cat in the history of the world. I have scratches to prove it."

"If it weren't for that cat, I would never have known to rescue you from the cellar," Flavia reminded him, returning her attention to their conversation. "You should be thanking him on bended knee. Though," she added. "I am reconsidering my position now I recall the cat entering my bedroom uninvited."

There was an awkward silence. "I never said he was likely to make a *good* husband," muttered Ygraine. "Which is no one's business but my own," she added.

"See," Orlando said, pointing at her. "You recognise his faults. Which is fine and just. If we had not caused the distraction we did, you would have gulped down a love philtre and even now be gushing at us about the perfection of your new husband's ear lobes, no matter whether he insults your mother or tups a dozen actresses on the other side of the river."

Ygraine stared open-mouthed at him. She managed somehow to achieve even this in a princessly manner. "Is that — I could never work out why you waited until *after* the ceremony to cause the hullabaloo. Why you hadn't stopped the wedding altogether."

"Would you have preferred that?" Orlando asked in a low voice.

The awkwardness was so thick that it could be served in slices with gravy.

A ball-bearing dropped suddenly from the top of the pavilion, twisting and rolling in a slow spiral around the domed roof, caught by rivulets and channels in the stone. It made a delicate chiming sound.

"That's our warning," said Ygraine. "The servants will be waking in half an hour."

"It still works," said Orlando with a boyish smile.

"You've been gone months, not years," Ygraine said irritably. "Everything works. The entire palace hums along to the whirring gears of the miraculous feats of engineering built into the very walls by the Extraordinary and Miraculous Device Brothers. Every time a meal is delivered by miniature steam train, or a guest discovers the rolling staircases for the first time, my family is reminded all over again of the reason behind the humiliating absence of my husband." She took a deep, shaky breath. "You haven't done anything horrid to him, have you?"

"No!" Orlando said, shocked at the idea. "We could have transformed Cornwall back on the spot without all the shouting and chaos. Then your mother had us locked up in the Tower of London..."

Ygraine frowned. "How *did* you escape? She warded those cells specially to impede your sparks."

"Yes," said Orlando with a dirty look in reply. "We did notice how long those particular wards had been in place. One thing you can say about the Queen, she likes to be prepared."

Ygraine raised her eyebrows.

Orlando grumbled. "Cornwall, if you must know.

He turned up at our window. Rinaldo was able to use his magic to break through the wards..."

"Archie travelled from Buckingham Palace to the Tower of London as a cat?" Ygraine said in surprise.

"Resourceful *and* bad-tempered," agreed Orlando. "Aren't you the pair?"

Ygraine shot him a glare that was somehow both wounded and threatening; Flavia admired the complexity.

"Anyway," Orlando went on. "We always planned to fix him. We needed somewhere warm and safe where we could work on it without being arrested again, and I remembered how Lady Mortmain had been trying to poach us from the Queen's service for years, and Rinaldo quite correctly said we probably shouldn't trust her." He looked miserable. "The first thing she did was take the cat hostage against our good behaviour... and we've been dancing to her tune ever since."

"Why turn him into a cat in the first place?"

"I didn't," Orlando snapped back at her. "I tried to transform the cup, to stop you drinking the love philtre. Everything that went wrong after that was because *I'm* wrong. My magic hasn't been right for years, and it's getting worse."

There was a long pause. Ygraine looked unexpectedly distraught. Finally, she asked in a more subdued voice: "Where is Archie now?"

"Ah," winced Orlando. "Miss Wednesday, could you explain this part?"

Flavia sighed, but at least this might get things moving along. "He's on the Isle of Faerie," she admitted.

Ygraine blinked. "Is that somewhere near Orkney?"

"No, *Faerie*. Where the fairies live since they were banished from the mortal world."

"By your ancestor, Good Queen Bess," Orlando added, to be helpful. "The one with the ruff."

"But," said Ygraine, turning it over in her mind. "But Mama hates fairies."

Orlando threw up his hands. "We didn't ask the Queen of Britannia's permission! It was —"

"Another terrible mistake," sighed the princess. "Yes, I understand. What's your plan?"

Orlando looked alarmed "My plan?"

"For returning my husband, you absurd creature."

"The plan is still in its early stages," Orlando confessed.

Flavia gave him a suspicious look. As far as she knew, the plan was simple — 1) collect the Water of Worlds from Buckingham Palace, 2) go to Faerie. What more could there be?

"So, you don't have a plan," said the princess. Her tone, more than anything else, sold the idea that she and Orlando had known each other since they were children.

"No need to worry," said Orlando brightly. "I'm sure Rinaldo will keep Cornwall alive. Or vice versa."

Ygraine leaned over and smacked him on the head. "Rinaldo? Have you lost your poor brother to the fairies too?"

Orlando looked sulky. "One could argue it was more his fault than mine."

"And now what?" the princess demanded. "How do you travel there to fetch them back? By boat?"

"There's a gate, but it is locked," said Flavia, thinking of the garden at Gloucester Worth. The winter solstice was still weeks away. They could not afford to wait for the Gate Sinister. Not with those children at the mercy of the Faerie Queen. Nothing happened in Faerie without Tanaquil Gloriana knowing all about it. She needed those children — or at least, their blood — to enact her plan to return to the mortal world.

"Actually," said Orlando. "I have samples of the magic philtres from the Forest of Arden, and that includes the Water of Worlds. If we isolate the philtre, I can produce more with an infernal machine such as the one that, uh, Rinaldo made for Lady Mortmain."

Now Flavia was the one glaring at him. She felt quite the double act with the princess. "*Isolate the philtre?* Don't you know which one it is?"

"I collected them in a hurry."

"But we can't wait. There's no time to lose."

"It won't take long," he said in what he probably thought was a soothing voice.

"Didn't it take Rinaldo weeks to make that machine at Actaeon Place? Do you even know how to replicate the philtre without him? You just told us your magic doesn't work properly."

"You can't use the workshop," said Ygraine, sounding hollow. "It's gone."

"I wasn't planning to —" Orlando looked gutted as her words caught up with him. "Gone?"

"Mama had it ripped out, destroyed. All of it. After you escaped the Tower. Every tool and cog. Papa's notebooks."

They stared at each other for a moment.

"Well," said Orlando, recovering with a bright, showman's smile. "I don't have to work on the philtres myself! This is the industrial age. Once we have consulted a certain Piccadilly alchemist of dubious morals with whom I am acquainted, everything will be coming up applesauce." He preened as if he had said something magnificent.

Flavia and Ygraine regarded him in shared concern.

"Are there no alchemists in Belgravia?" Ygraine asked after a moment.

"Their morals aren't dubious enough." Orlando leaped to his feet dramatically. "It's been splendid to exchange pleasantries with my favourite princess, but we have an alchemist to hire and some loved ones to rescue from bloodthirsty fairies. I'll bring the cat — I mean, the Duke — back to you as soon as I can."

Ygraine stood, staring at him from out of her silk hood with a piercing gaze. "No."

Orlando looked baffled. "You don't want him back?"

"Of course I want him back. This was my one chance to build a life for myself, and I am not going to let you ruin it. I don't trust you, Orlando Device."

He looked like a kicked puppy. "You used to trust me."

"Did I?" Ygraine replied, chilly as a frost fair. "What a child I must have been. I trust you to rescue your brother, but I don't believe you give a damn about anyone else." She said the word 'damn' very self-consciously, as if she had been practising it in the mirror. "I'm coming with you."

Orlando's mouth fell open. "We're heading up Piccadilly! There will be backstreets and taverns. That's hardly the place to take a lady."

Flavia coughed. "I suppose *I* was invited along on this expedition?"

Orlando gave her a blank look. "That's different. Governesses can go anywhere. Besides, I was going to leave you to wait for me in Hyde Park."

Flavia bridled at that. "Leave me? Like a parcel?"

"Piccadilly is hardly Whitechapel," Ygraine insisted. "I know it well."

"Taking tea in private houses or shopping in the

finer boutiques, chaperoned by an army of maids," Orlando said dismissively. "I leave the princessing to you, please leave the shady alchemists to me."

"I have a hood. I'm wearing sensible boots, no jewels," said Ygraine, standing her ground. "I have been waiting for you or your brother to return for *months*, and I have standing orders with my maid to cover for me for at least a day and a half should I disappear unexpectedly."

Orlando gave her a sceptical look. "What are you wearing under that opera cloak?"

"Sacque and combing jacket," she said with a sweet smile, describing the kind of private garment a lady would never be caught wearing in public. Flavia instantly recognised it as sarcasm. Orlando was too worked up to realise.

"Ygraine, your mother would murder me!"

"I'm wearing a sensible dress, actually," she sighed. "I told you, I've prepared for this. I would have caught you the first time you stashed your little parcel in that trees, but Mama and I were taking tea with the Maharajah Singh and his wife and I couldn't get away."

The princess had clearly put more thought into her escape than Orlando had ever in his life put into anything. Flavia didn't care if she came or not, only that they got moving. "I suppose I count as an appropriate chaperone," she said impatiently.

"There is no way I am dragging two gentlewomen through the taverns of London," Orlando declared.

The futility of his statement was conveyed perfectly by the twin stares of disdain that both Flavia and Ygraine cast upon him. Flavia rather liked having an ally in sensible decision-making, and Ygraine darted her a small smile that suggested she felt the same.

Orlando groaned. "Queen Isolda is going to set her dogs on me."

"I wouldn't worry," said Ygraine briskly. "She has been wanting to set the dogs on you for months. Nothing you do now can possibly prevent it."

~

Rinaldo ran.

First, he was following the cat.

The blur of yellow darted in and out of the trees, taunting them and pulling them in closer, daring them to get themselves lost. It flitted from tree to tree like it was a butterfly. A vengeful, angry butterfly.

There was no 'them.' He had lost Queenie. That was the first disaster.

Sweat clung to his collar and dampened his hair. He was not used to this kind of sticky heat.

The second disaster came when Rinaldo finally cornered the cat between two trees in the strange-smelling forest. (The trees smelled of oranges and spices and something else he could not quite put his finger on.) He crept slowly towards his prey, then pounced and grabbed... only for the yellow feline to disappear suddenly in a ribbon of smoke that giggled as it slid emptily through Rinaldo's fingers.

Faerie. If he had been unsure before, now he knew exactly where they were. He had been chasing a phantom, a will o' the wisp. For all he knew, Queenie was following the real cat, or had been lured away by a different wisp.

The lack of metal was affecting Rinaldo's mind. This land was all growing things, sprouts and branches and grasses, nothing real he could hang on to.

It was worse than being trapped in the Tower of London, inside wards; there was nothing standing between him and his magic, only an absence of anything like fuel for his sparks.

Rinaldo turned back the way he had come and found himself facing a ghost.

Princess Ygraine. Not the furious harridan in a wedding dress as he had last seen her, screaming as he and Orlando fled the ballroom...

No, this was Ygraine at seventeen, her hair pinned up under a tiara for her birthday ball. She wore a pearl-encrusted cloud of a gown. They danced the waltz together, and no one even tutted with disapproval...

She didn't look tired and happy now, though. She looked wan, as if she had walked across a desert to get here. "Rinaldo," she said.

"Are you all right? How are you here?" He stepped

forward, set a hand on her arm and felt her skin warm underneath.

She was real. Real enough. Not a wisp. But that only raised more questions.

"Tell me something," he demanded. "Prove you are the real Ygraine."

The princess tipped her face up to his, looking miserable. "Does he even know?" she breathed.

Ygraine

sister of Princess Oonagh, Duchess of Scarborough

In talking about the Device brothers, I skipped over a few years including Evanna's marriage to the Earl of Orkney, and Oonagh's to the Duke of Scarborough — both happened when I was nine, while we were all still in mourning for Papa.

The Queen choosing to marry off two of her daughters so close to home was not popular. Palace courtiers muttered about the lost chance to make diplomatic ties abroad. Even Cousin Victoria, who usually knew how to keep her head down, came to Mama with a list of suitable European princes and noblemen; after being rebuked, Victoria arranged for her own daughters to marry them instead.

Evanna and Oonagh had sombre weddings. Mama insisted they marry in black to honour our late father, rather than the family tradition of green.

Our sister Iseult's tragic death, and the short, sharp war with Eire that occurred thereafter, occupied the three months between Evanna's wedding, and Oonagh's. We were in mourning all over again by the time the Duke and Duchess of Scarborough served their wedding breakfast in a sea of black silk.

There were no fairy costumes or flower-bedecked tables, though Oonagh had craved them wildly. The wedding breakfast was small and respectful, and then Oonagh was whisked away to her new life.

I had no thoughts in my head about the Duke of Scarborough except that, as with my other sisters, Oonagh's bridegroom seemed old.

When the worst happened, a year later, it appeared in the London newspapers before we were told at Buckingham Palace. All I knew at first was that the servants were terrified, whispering in corners and staring at the family.

Uncle Albert and Cousin Victoria took me to their rooms, I recall. My favourite cousin Louise, only a year younger than Oonagh, fed me cakes, and let me use her best pencils until I fell asleep.

Unity came to fetch me eventually: a tall and sulky fifteen-year-old who resented me for being the baby of the family. "Oonagh's dead," she said briefly. "Don't cry in front of Mama, she has enough to deal with."

I had not exchanged a word with Mama for months; she had taken the hit of Iseult's death with grim silence. Somehow it was *Oonagh's* death that woke her up out of her mourning fog. Still wrapped in black like a majestic crow, she returned to work with a new zeal, ready to conquer every country and shore up every colony that she could. It was as if she had resigned herself to inevitable personal tragedy in all her daughters and pushed all future grief aside in order to be, well...

The Empress of Britannia. I'm sure you've seen the portraits, read the speeches. She's on the coins.

Mama's mask never cracked again. She accepted the news of the safe birth of Evanna's firstborn son Gawain with steely indifference.

I had no idea what had happened to Oonagh, for the longest time. I had heard about Iseult and her Tristan from eavesdropping on servants, cousins and my surviving sisters, but everyone was closed-lipped about the Duchess of Scarborough's untimely end.

What I did notice — what nobody could fail to notice — was that Mama was not only obsessed with her colonies and her imperial might. She had also embarked upon a campaign against fairies.

Faerie fashion was quite the thing in the 1860s, thanks to several popular periodicals publishing sketches of Iseult's wedding. Young ladies all around Britannia had been adding silk leaves and gossamer wings to their formal gowns for years. Girls of my sisters' age, raised on the *Dear Little Acorn* tales by Miss Primula Millicent Wednesday, were now wildly infatuated with Christina Rossetti, Blake, Yeats... any poet willing to write about the Isle of Faerie, the Forest of Arden, or the Age of Chivalry.

It's amazing all the young men weren't parading up and down Bond Street in chainmail.

Oonagh's gowns were all like that, before her wedding. Silver and pale green, with enormous bustles covered in lace like cobwebs, and patterns of silken petals. She always refused Mama's diamond tiara and wore roses in her hair instead.

When I picture her, she looks like a water colour illustration in a book of Tennyson.

The Empress of Britannia came out kicking after Oonagh's death, and she claimed the arts as one of her weapons. She had portraits and plays commissioned about Good Queen Bess, reminding Britannia that we banished the fairies from the land for good reason.

Whenever Arwenna and Unity appeared in public, it was in Elizabethan-style ruffs paired with stiffened lace. Their bustles could be decorated with ribbon and beads, never cobwebs or petals.

Any girl coming out that season was warned against appearing too 'pastoral' when presented to the Queen.

I realised it was about more than fashion when my cousin Louise gave me a copy of the newly released *Bulfinch's Mythology* for my tenth birthday, and Mama confiscated it from my hands.

"Even Shakespeare wrote about fairies!" complained Louise, who had many bohemian friends, and knew artists whose livelihoods had been damaged by this swift move away from the romantic fairy aesthetic.

Mama went stone still, and Cousin Victoria hurried her children away to their little retreat on the Isle of Wight; Louise was not welcome at Buckingham Palace for months afterwards.

I burned to know what had happened to Oonagh. What could be so bad that it made Mama want to change the world? What did it have to do with the fashion for fairy frocks and wings?

Eventually, I found a stash of old newspapers, put aside by the footmen on days when the front pages were not to be shown to the family, and I pieced it together for myself.

Love philtres again: a wicked man who wanted something he did not deserve. In this case, it was an enchanter who had slipped a philtre to the newly married Duchess of Scarborough while her husband was away, and spent the night in her bed.

(The newspapers drew a veil over what happened during that night, though I was old enough to know it wasn't the done thing for married ladies to share a bed with men who were not their husband.)

The enchanter played a cruel game with Oonagh, asking impossible tasks of her as if they were characters in one of those fairy tales she loved. To make him a cambric shirt without a seam. To pick him a rose without a thorn. Riddles, quests, like this was a grand romance, not blackmail.

I don't know what she was thinking. I don't know why she asked no one for help. But that's the thing about a love philtre: it takes away everything but the person you adore.

She fought it; I never knew she had such strength, but she did. When the enchanter gave her a poison to put in the cup of her returning husband, Oonagh swallowed it herself.

She left a journal behind: endless letters half gibberish, half poetry, explaining what had happened. The newspapers got hold of them, somehow, and printed whole tracts in her handwriting.

Now I knew why Mama had declared war on fairy tales. I'd rather lost the taste for them myself.

I dreamed of fairies, the night after I first learned of Oonagh's fate. I still dream of them, sometimes.

I dream of a house of flowers, and a golden grail, and a green-skinned girl gazing at me like I'm worth kissing.

I dread that one day, the fairy tales are going to find me.

One began to weave a crown
Of tendrils, leaves, and rough nuts brown
(Men sell not such in any town);
One heaved the golden weight
Of dish and fruit to offer her:
"Come buy, come buy," was still their cry.
Laura stared but did not stir,
Longed but had no money:
The whisk-tailed merchant bade her taste
In tones as smooth as honey...

— Christina Rossetti, *Goblin Market*,
1862

Chapter 3

In Which Annie Apples Has Her Own Ideas On the Matter

At dawn, the creaky market-carts toiled slowly along the thoroughfare at Hyde Park Corner, laden with produce destined for Covent Garden. Fresh cabbages and onions, carrots and potatoes, shining and damp, gleamed from every cart. They had been out of the earth a few hours at most.

The wide street had a rustic look to it, nothing like the parade of swells and flower-hatted maidens that usually decorated such a grand park. It was too early for the fine families to be awake. At dawn, London belonged to those who fed and clothed the city, not to those who had the most money to spend. The grand buildings towering over the horses and carts remained silent and still, peopled only by sleeping aristocrats, and their quiet but industrious servants.

Farmers and drivers guided the horses and carts this way and that, gathering manure when it fell, so it could be taken to the crops when the morning's work was done.

Ygraine, Duchess of Cornwall and Land's End, walked as if she was not out of place, though the shimmering midnight blue silk of her cloak did not belong to this time of day. She looked like a fine lady who had lost her way after the opera, and not yet returned home.

Flavia, accustomed to sliding under the notice of crowds, *felt* every odd look darted at them from the busy workers.

Orlando strode up the street with a whistle, confident in his tailored coat top hat to provide him with a status beyond question, despite his Chinese face. His easy stride led Flavia and their hooded royal companion to a coffee stall in the corner of Hyde Park. They drank from tin cups along with the city clerks and shopgirls on their way to their own employment.

Flavia had never felt so tired in her life, and the bitter coffee did little to replace the night's sleep she had suffered without. But she could not stop to rest, not with the Gloucester children at the mercy of the fairies. Besides, she had nowhere to safely lay her head. Sleeping under a bush in the park might sound like a marvellous way to refresh her magic and be at one with the greenery, but it would leave her rather vulnerable to contact from her mother.

"Do alchemists rise so early?" she asked as they left the coffee stall behind and walked along Piccadilly: one of the widest and straightest streets in London. The street was lined with mansion houses and elegant hotels, though none of them showed any signs of life. After a long stretch, they passed a row of beautiful shops readying themselves for the business day.

"Let's find him first," said Orlando. "Then we can worry if it's too early to shake him awake."

Princess Ygraine gave him a sharp-eyed look from beneath her sweeping hood. "Is this where the taverns come in?"

"I'm not such a reprobate as you think," Orlando chided her. "The best way to find most information fast happens to be asking around in public houses. Which is why I was not planning to bring a pair of judge-mental young ladies along for the day trip." He frowned at Ygraine's feet, where dainty buttoned boots peeped out from under her long skirt and sweeping cloth. "I'm not sure your shoe leather is up to today's proceedings."

"Let's not argue," said Flavia. "How far away is this your public house of yours?"

This end of Piccadilly, while it had as much mud and dust from carriages as any other street in the city, could surely not offer establishments seedy enough for Orlando's purposes. It seemed unlikely the fine gentlemen and ladies who arrived here in their phaetons to pay calls or to purchase gowns would not stop off for a swift half along the way. Or if they did, it would be in the kind of exclusive club that would never allow Flavia (or Orlando, come to think of it) over the threshold.

"I'd get there faster alone," Orlando said, in a wheedling manner. "If any ladies of my acquaintance wanted to give up now, and any other ladies of my acquaintance were willing to chaperone them back home, I might be able to scrounge the fare for a cab."

He was sensible at least to leave words such as 'princess' and 'palace' out of his vocabulary in public.

Ygraine gave him a chilly look, worthy of young Queenie Gloucester at her most offended. "I have spooned soup for the poor and wrapped bandages in a volunteer hospital. I think I can manage a tavern or two without requiring a fainting couch."

"Oh yes," said Flavia under her breath as they followed in Orlando's wake. "They do so love to be called the poor."

Orlando knew where he was going. After a long hike along the main sweep of Piccadilly, he drew the ladies with him into narrower streets and squares, taking every turn as if he knew exactly what he would find around that corner.

Shops were squashed closer together here, and there were public houses on nearly every block, though none open this early in the morning. There were purveyors of all manner of goods and services, from sweets and cakes to tailoring and antiques, alongside booksellers, and little offices for solicitors or doctors. The narrower the streets became, the less fancy the shop windows, though oddly the windows became cleaner as the items for sale became less grand.

In a small green square surrounded by white-washed apartments, Orlando finally called a halt outside a public house with a sign proclaiming it The Green Horn. Also on the sign was a badly painted cornucopia... the strategic placement of two large peaches making it very clear that a dirty joke was intended.

Flavia kept her face straight. One didn't get to be a professional governess without a preternatural ability to ignore innuendo.

The Green Horn was slightly more respectable than Flavia had imagined, but only because the front step had been recently washed. Also, the tavern was closed so there were no customers to make the place look untidy.

Orlando marched around the shabby building, disappearing into a narrow alley. "Come along, ladies," he called. "This is what you wanted, isn't it? To rough it with the plebs."

"I imagined we'd be going in through the front door," Ygraine said in a low voice.

Flavia gave her a companionable smile which came out as more of a wince.

Behind the Green Horn was a yard littered with empty barrels. Orlando set to waking the occupants, rattling the windows and calling out in a loud voice "Ho the Horn! Who's still sleeping? Up and at 'em."

Flavia had visions of them being chased out of the
yard by an angry innkeeper the size and shape of a bull.
The princess had frozen with embarrassment beside
her, doing a good job of impersonating a statue.

A window slammed open from the top floor, and a
doxy in a low-cut chemise (or a respectable woman
still in her night-things, it was always so difficult to tell
the difference) leaned out, still fixing pins into her
wild golden hair. "Who's calling there?" she cried out
in a broad Eirish accent. "We serve no beer until the
sun's past the yard-arm, so run along home, ye
wasters!"

"Sweet Annie Apples," said Orlando with a grin
that lit his face up beautifully. He capered back a step
or two so she could see him properly, and placed both
hands over his heart. "Will you not do a favour for an
old friend?"

The wench caught her breath and laughed down at
him. "Jay —" she started to say but swallowed the
sound quickly. "Why, Orlando Device, is that you
lurking around my barrels, you smooth-talking devil? I
thought you to be hanged by now."

Flavia watched their mutual performance in
fascination.

"The day is young, there's still time," Orlando said
with a wink for Ygraine, who buried her own expres-
sionless face deep inside her hood. "Let us in, will you,
sweet-heart?"

"Only for a few minutes," Annie said with a sigh.

"I've a day to be getting on with, and no time for your frummery."

A moment later, the Eirishwoman unlatched the back of the tavern and let the three of them inside. With a sturdy brown day dress flung over the chemise, and a bleached white apron over that, she looked perfectly respectable after all, though her golden hair still tangled about her shoulders. She embraced Orlando like a sister and squawked at him when he squeezed her too familiarly. "No sauce, you! My John will pound you into the walls if you give him half a reason."

"Ladies," Orlando said to Flavia and Ygraine. "May I present Annie Apples, a dear friend from my misspent youth. She's the landlady of the Green Horn."

"Is it rooms you're wanting?" Mrs Apples asked, eyeing Flavia and Ygraine with a dubious air, as if their very proximity to Orlando rendered them unworthy of her freshly scrubbed tavern.

Flavia thought about commenting that Orlando, barely into his twenties, was surely still in the middle of his misspent youth rather than leaving it behind him, but she couldn't quite find the strength. The long night and the longer walk caught up with her all at once, as if her body recognised this as a safe place to land.

"All I need's a bite of gossip, lovely," said Orlando, his accent roughening around the edges as he focused his attention on his friend. "I need a word with

Cavendish the pot-stirrer, is he around? He used to have that shop over in St James's Square, but I found it boarded up."

"That rogue," said Mrs Apples with a scoffing noise. "I threw him out o' here three nights ago for groping barmaids. He sells his wares on a tray up Covent Garden way, since the shop was taken off him by the landlord's boys. Not sure what use he'll be to you, man. Do you not know any sober alchemists?"

"Never met one yet," Orlando said with a grin. "Any chance of a bite of breakfast before you send us on our merry way?"

"And not a penny to pay for it, I expect," Mrs Apples said in a huff. She looked more closely at Flavia. "I'll feed this one, sure. What have you done to the poor lass, Orlando? She looks ready to keel over."

"I'm fine," said Flavia, tugging the thick coat more closely around her. "I'm only..."

To her extreme embarrassment, her feet disappeared from under her.

~

Does he even know? One minute, Rinaldo was gaping at the princess for saying something so cruel, and the next Ygraine had stepped forward into his arms as if she expected to pick up their dance where they had left off, three years ago.

He stepped back quickly. "No, thank you."

Ygraine wrinkled her nose, as she used to when the Device brothers rattled off technical terms she didn't understand. "I'm not what you want?"

His aghast look must have said it all; she stepped back, looking even more confused. Then her face cleared. "Ah. This is the one, then."

Ygraine's figure thickened, her chin lifted, and her dark hair spiralled into a fair braid. One arm stretched, becoming braided leaves and flowers instead of skin. "Kiss me," said Flavia Wednesday, launching herself in his general direction.

Rinaldo recoiled so hard he backed into a tree. "Who are you?" he demanded. "What do you want?"

Flavia threw up her arms and pouted, an expression that belonged nowhere on the governess's face. "I've never worked so hard for a kiss," she protested.

The air around them was thick and sweet and hot; it made it rather hard to think sensibly. "I don't want to kiss you," said Rinaldo.

"Obviously!" said the not-Flavia, throwing up arms that were the wrong proportions — too long, too narrow. Grass and loose clover fanned through the air. She shrank into a small, lithe creature whose face was covered in a mask of dandelion clocks. Bright eyes, sharp teeth. "You're not even worth the prize," the creature grumbled.

Somewhere, a woman laughed.

Rinaldo turned away from the shape-changing sprite and saw a vision on horseback approaching him.

Lady Elspeth Mortmain, one of the most dangerous enchantresses in all Britannia, sat astride a silver palfrey. Her long golden hair was down in curls around her waist instead of pinned up in fashionable restraint. Last time he saw her she was wearing widow's black and a sturdy leather apron; somewhere among the sprites and meadows, she had located a dress shop. She was draped a long white gown like something from a Waterhouse painting, all soft muslin and curves. No sign of a corset, or shoes.

Behind her, the sun glowed as if it was a hair away from sunset, though Rinaldo could have sworn it was morning only a few moments ago.

"They're getting even further off track," Rinaldo muttered. "I wouldn't kiss this one to save my life."

"They won't stop trying to catch you out," said the enchantress, highly amused. "Kisses are their main currency, and worth more if they trick you into it."

Rinaldo shielded his eyes from the setting sun, wondering if it was really her or another hoax. "You've made yourself comfortable around here," he noted.

Lady Mortmain laughed again. "I've known Faerie a long time," she replied. "I'm comfortable in the terrain."

Rinaldo frowned. They'd just arrived. Hadn't they? "How long have you been here?"

"How long is a night's sleep? How long is a piece of

string?" She gave him an arch look. "Sooner or later they'll realise you can't be seduced, Mr Device. I did."

Ha. Rinaldo's disinterest in Lady Mortmain — or kisses in general — hadn't slowed her plans for a minute, not when there was Orlando to manipulate. "Can they see inside my mind?" They had got that picture of Ygraine from somewhere — and they knew that Flavia meant something to him, even if they made a whole lot of assumptions along the way.

"They can see into your dreams, which isn't quite the same thing. Shadows and reflections. But they're simple creatures. They assume all humans are the same, that we all want to tup and lick and cram our bellies with their fruits." Lady Mortmain shook her golden hair back into the dying sunshine. "That's their mistake," she said confidently.

"Accepted you as their queen yet, have they?" Rinaldo said sarcastically, remembering her 'Queen Elspeth the First' speech from the attic. This was an enchantress with ambition.

She laughed again, a cruel and tinkling sound as she turned her steed away from him. "They will, Mr Device. And where will you be, then?"

~

When Flavia returned to her senses, she was sitting in a sturdy chair in the corner of a shabby but comfortable kitchen. Almost as soon as she shook herself clear of the daze, a warm cup of porridge and honey was placed in her hands.

"Eat that up, child," said Mrs Apples in a kind voice.

Flavia stared up at the landlady. They could not be more than a year or two apart, for all of Annie's coarse skin and motherly manner. The porridge smelled for a moment like it came from Mrs Brundage's kitchen and that made Flavia want to cry. "I feel so stupid. I haven't slept. It was a busy night."

"You've been stretched thin for more than one night, my treasure, if I know anything about anything," said the landlady in a stern voice. She sounded like she was at least as old as Mrs Brundage, though she couldn't be much older than Flavia herself.

"We're disturbing you in your work, Mrs..."

"Call me Evanna, never mind Orlando and his Annie Apples nonsense. I remember when he was plain old James and I ain't never mocked him for changing it. Don't worry about my work. If there's any sweeping to be done before the punters come in for their ale and cider, Mr High and Mighty Lives in a Palace Device can do it himself."

"You're very kind," said Flavia, and began to eat the

porridge, one shaky spoonful at a time. She knew better than to insult someone who was trying to feed her.

She was halfway through the cup when Orlando stuck his head back into the kitchen. "I've got your water pump working again, my love. If I had a spare afternoon I could run back here and clap a steam engine to it, get you hot running water in the kitchen..."

"And likely blow my public house up to kingdom come," Evanna said with a laugh. "Don't you go fixing one of your witch-engines to anything that's mine."

"I'm hurt and wounded at your lack of trust," Orlando smirked. He eased himself all the way into the kitchen, rolling his sleeves back down and looking around for his coat. "How are you holding up, Miss Wednesday? I've led you quite a dance. I understand if it's too much for your feet."

He was far more deferential than Flavia was used to, and that only made her suspicious. "You're not leaving me behind," she said, setting the cup down.

"Never said I would. The market will be teeming now, all the better to close in on our rabbit before he gets a chance to hop away." Orlando turned and gave Evanna a hug that was mostly squeeze. They buzzed each other briefly on the lips. "Thanks for the breakfast, my heart."

"I don't like the sound of any of this," Evanna frowned, tugging at what remained of his cravat and managing somehow to make him look slightly more respectable. "You need our Rinaldo to stop you hurtling into the most reckless adventures."

"The professor spoils most of my fun," Orlando agreed. "But look, I brought a governess along instead! She'll keep me out of the worst scrapes."

That was a high responsibility, and one that Flavia hadn't entirely volunteered for. The sooner Rinaldo Device was back in this world, the better. She was certain she did not have the moral strength to play his part as Orlando's reins and conscience rolled together for more than a short while.

Evanna Apples gave Orlando an unimpressed look. "And what do I say when the Queen herself sends the peelers after her lost lamb? If I'm to be dragged away to the stocks for housing a kidnapper *and* a runaway princess, I'd like to be prepared."

He blinked, caught out. "I don't ..."

"I'm no fool, Orlando Device. Do you think I've never stood under that balcony at Buckingham Palace, waving my flag at the royal family? I'm a Britannian, and I know a princess when I see one." Evanna gave him a push to be on his way. "Rid yourself of her as fast as you can, or she'll see you hanged before the week is out."

"I'm afraid it's a matter of honour," said Orlando. "Temporarily. Nothing to be done."

Evanna shook her head at him. "Get it sorted and get that princess back where she belongs or you'll bring a world of trouble down on your head," she pronounced. "I won't be the one to explain to Rinaldo how you got your fool self killed."

~

Rinaldo found his way back to the river; or perhaps it was another river. The bank was lined with buttercups that glowed like gold coins. It was morning again, though he did not remember sleeping.

It had been sunset, and now it was morning.

They can see into your dreams, Lady Mortmain had teased him, or warned him. How could you dream in a place where sleep did not exist?

He had to get through this. Had to collect Queenie, and her brother. Had to find that bloody cat...

Rinaldo was so thirsty he could not think. He plunged his hands into the river and brought them up as a cup to drink from. *Don't eat or drink in fairyland, or you'll be trapped forever*, he vaguely remembered from books, but that never sounded especially scientific to him.

Don't drink anything that might be a philtre... not exactly helpful to a man dying of thirst.

He should have read more books. All that time he lived as a Royal Engineer at Buckingham Palace, with access to one of the greatest private libraries in the world. He had immersed himself in the reference works that were of relevance to his craft: of science and philosophy, mathematics and magical engineering. He had never bothered to revisit the fairy tales and chivalric myths that so enchanted him when he was young and books were scarce.

A good fat reference tome about fairies and their customs would be exceedingly useful about now.

Rinaldo pushed his hands into the cold water again. This time, he felt something rough and strange under his hands, like wet linen from a gentleman's shirt. He hauled it upwards, and a body came with it: a body almost as familiar as his own, in soaking wet clothes, with wild black hair flowering like a dandelion in the water.

Orlando.

Orlando dead.

Does he even know?

Ygraine

and the Sparks of Buckingham Palace

I was twelve when Uncle Albert's bad stomach finally got the better of him. He died slowly over two weeks of prolonged misery. It was like losing Papa all over again. I hadn't spent as much time in the workshop over the last two years, but I still felt his loss keenly.

Everyone leaves a legacy, I suppose. An imprint of the work they did in life, the things they valued and made and shaped. Albert's legacy — well, to the world it was Crystal Palace, the delight that the Britannian people took in the Great Exhibition of 1851 (before I was born, and weren't my sisters insufferable about how they got to go and I did not).

For me, his legacy was Buckingham Palace. Albert had left his fingerprints all over it, with the assistance of Papa's old notebooks, and the orphaned sparks he dragged in off the street.

Every stair in Buckingham Palace was now automated, gliding with no trace of clunk. We had mechanised lifts that not only carried food swiftly from kitchen to dining room (piping hot meals for the first time in my life!) but also transported trunks and furniture from floor to floor.

Statues that moved and danced and seemed at times to breathe were displayed in every niche, nook or courtyard, including the majestic figure of Good Queen Bess in all her glory. Mechanical sailing ships swooped back and forth across the ornamental lake in the grounds. We had steam-powered devices for drying hands and hair in every bathroom. (I always thought of Uncle Albert in winter when my feet landed on the toasty floor.)

Buckingham Palace had been a dreary place to grow up, far too cold and damp when one was not being Grand for Guests. While Mama was busy with her affairs of state, the palace had become truly marvellous: an everyday miracle.

All thanks to Uncle Albert.

Cousin Victoria could not stop crying; we had little hope she would recover from her loss as robustly as Mama (eventually) had.

After the endless processional funeral, Mama hosted a family gathering at Buckingham Palace. To my surprise — to everyone's surprise — she invited the shabby Device brothers to leave their oily, steam-bathed workshop and join the family for tea and finger sandwiches.

They came, Orlando and Rinaldo both uncomfortable in formal suits that had never been worn. They had been provided with anything they needed once Uncle Albert moved them in here, but always at his direction, under his supervision.

Their protector was gone.

My surviving sisters were all here for the funeral — Evanna, Arwenna and Unity. It was rare to see Evanna, who had buried herself in her life on Orkney, while Arwenna was constantly visiting since her own wedding to the Earl of Dorset. Unity was frustrated at being stranded in London an extra four weeks for the funeral events, postponing her journey towards the Bavarian prince she was to wed. (Mama had reluctantly allowed a foreign alliance this time, though it took months of agonised negotiations and upset her whole notion of presenting her family as entirely *Britannian*.)

My sisters threw the occasional pitying look in the direction of the Device brothers, so out of place in our stiff little soiree. Otherwise they ignored them, as did the rest of the family. Grandfather Cormac, now pale and paper-thin, peered at Orlando and Rinaldo in confusion but thankfully asked no offensive questions about their presence.

Cousin Victoria wept, surrounded by those of her children who had been able to travel home in time. She hadn't a thought in her head for the children her husband had dragged into their home to make his work easier; why should she?

Rinaldo looked like he might hurl himself out of a window from sheer embarrassment. Orlando looked like he longed to disassemble every clock in the room (and immediately thereafter, leave the room in search of more clocks).

I resented those two sparks, deeply. But somehow, seeing them in their starchy collars, wishing for exile from the formal gathering, all I could think of was how delighted Uncle Albert was every time one of them did something clever.

I marched over, picked up a plate of sandwiches and thrust it directly under the noses of the Device brothers.

"Shall we withdraw to the library?" I offered. It came out rather demanding, but they might as well get used to that.

Rinaldo's eyes lit up beneath his heavy brows. "Yes, *please*," he said.

Orlando reached over to take three sandwiches. "Anywhere not in this room would be excellent," he said before stuffing them in his mouth.

I hurried them out of the reception room before any of my sisters noticed I was smiling.

The library of Buckingham Palace was my newest
refuge, after these two stole the workshop. I loved the
window seats, deep bookcases and the odd little nooks
here and there where it was possible to hide for hours
with a novel and a bag of toffees if, for example, one's
sister was rampaging about a mislaid foundation
garment which may or may not have been tossed on top
of a wardrobe where she would never think to look
for it.

"I'm sure they'll remember you exist, sooner or
later," I observed, sitting in a window seat and tucking
my black dress around my legs to be modest. Orlando
placed the platter of sandwiches atop a teetering stack
of fairy stories bound in fine gold-tipped editions.

(The sugary tales of Primula Millicent Wednesday;
I hoped they didn't think I read such nonsense.)

"I'd rather they didn't remember us at all," said
Rinaldo, his eyes roaming a nearby shelf of atlases as if
he was hungrier for those than sandwiches. "Do you
think we can stay in here until they decide what to do
with us? Five or six years would be about right."

Oh. Of course, they would be worried about being
sent back to the orphanage, or wherever it was that
Uncle Albert had found them.

"Don't mind him," said Orlando, hopping up on
the window seat as if I was a perfectly ordinary girl.
"The professor here goes giddy at the smell of paper.

We won't get anything sensible out of him for hours. My condolences and all that," he added, somewhat awkwardly. "Mr Albert was always talking about you. I reckon you were his favourite."

I would not cry. "He wasn't a Mister," I snapped, blinking my eyelashes hard. "He was a Britannian Duke. A Germanian Prince. He was brought over here to marry my mother, but they didn't take to each other, and Cousin Victoria liked him so much that she married him instead." She smiled sadly. "If Mama had not survived childhood, Cousin Victoria would have been queen and Albert her king."

"He would have made a good king," Orlando said gravely.

I felt a small tear sniffle into place above my nose and wiped it away.

"Rubbish," Rinaldo interrupted from where was sorting through a shelf of scientific journals as if they were the most enticing sugared almonds. "He would have been a disaster. No one wants a king who spends his whole reign building contraptions and inviting famous scientists to the palace so he can pick their brains. Mr Albert was excellent engineer, that's better than a king."

"He could have done both," Orlando said rebelliously. "Being king hardly takes up all the hours in the day."

I laughed, my tears disappearing. "You're right," I admitted. "He would have made a terrible king!"

How irritating. I now found myself entirely on their side. And if these rotten little sparks needed a new protector in Buckingham Palace, with Uncle Albert gone...

It would have to be me, wouldn't it?

By 1875, the Britannian public's taste for lurid tales about the tragic fates of their royal princesses waned. Interest in the Royal Family was greatly revived when Princess Ygraine was publicly betrothed to Viscount Lyon (Archibalt Lyonesse, later the Duke of Cornwall and Land's End) on her seventeenth birthday.

As the Queen became more distracted with her campaigns of imperial conquest, it was left to Ygraine to represent the Royal family in public. She did so with a fierce zeal that elevated the three years between her engagement and eventual wedding into a fresh and vibrant era for Society.

Princess Ygraine's every public appearance was raked over with an obsessive eye, and her dress choices steered popular fashion in an entirely new direction.

Gone were the crinolettes and bustles that characterised the public image of her older sisters: Ygraine preferred a tailored silhouette, flattening the back of still-sumptuous gowns which fell in ruffles or gathers from the hip instead of the waist in a cascading style that became known as 'princess dress.'

As noted by various fashion historians, the palette preferred by this princess changed significantly depending on whether her outfit was likely to come to the attention of her mother: at public events involving the monarch, the princess dressed in Isolda's preferred signature colours of black and green. When Princess Ygraine attended events in her own right, she was often spotted in bolder shades: mulberry and deep blue were among her favourites.

See Fig 8. The Phèdre Opera Cloak, worn by the princess at the opening night of Sarah Bernhardt's first London tour and immortalised in a sketch on the front cover of La Belle Assemblée.

— Professor Lucy Rhodes-Carmody,
Queenly Wardrobes, 2024

Chapter 4

In Which Alchemists Can Be Cheaply Bought

Princess Ygraine awaited them in the yard outside the Green Horn, her hood settled back into place, and heavy band of Piccadilly grime and dust weighing down the hem of her midnight silk cloak. "Shall we go?" she said in a brisk voice.

"Next stop, Covent Garden," replied Orlando, far too cheerful about it.

More walking. Flavia at least felt fortified from her short nap and her cup of porridge. She had no idea what was fuelling Orlando.

He led them forth through more London streets, past a slew of gentleman's clubs and hat shops. The iron in the air and in fences, door locks and window latches they passed gave Flavia a headache, but there was the occasional strip of green here or there to give her some relief along the way.

Covent Garden came as an overwhelming relief. The air felt sweet again. Flowers and vegetables, trees and herbs, everything a fairy needed to survive in the middle of the largest city in Britannia.

Flavia was no stranger to markets. Her childhood in her great-aunt's cottage had been a constant whirl of bottling and preserving, stirring and sugaring, all in preparation for the Tipwell Village Market on Thursdays, when she and Great-Aunt Petula Millicent Wednesday sold jars of chutney, pickles, sugared violets and rose petals, elderflower cordial and apples-in-brandy. Market sales contributed as much to their modest living as the occasional bank note sent down from London by the publisher of those sweet little fairy stories.

Even the word 'market' now brought the taste of cherry wine to her tongue. The smell had clung to the cottage walls and curtains for days after brewing. Flavia knew the hum and beat of a good produce market like she knew the true shade of her own green skin.

She had never seen anything like Covent Garden.

It was a city all of its own, a sprawling citadel of flower sellers and farmers, a grand temple to Flora and Pomona, the ancient Greek goddesses of plenty. Its central avenue, enclosed by high roof of steel (ugh, always steel, but a good distance away) and glass, was lush with all manner of expensive and beautiful produce.

Flavia could smell the dirt of a dozen counties, a rich and earthy smell that made her want to plant her feet and sway like a willow tree.

The morning's work was well underway, and the market was 'teeming' as Orlando had predicted. There were almost as many customers as vegetables: cooks, kitchen maids and housekeepers with baskets on their arms, top-hatted gentlemen, rough and ready drivers and hollering shopkeepers. The flower hall was a draw for ladies' maids, housekeepers and hotel staff, selecting bright blooms to decorate tables, reception desks, and private homes.

Plants were for sale in the conservatory — this was the area Flavia most longed to explore. There was nothing as beautiful to her as green things growing, and now that the porridge had settled her stomach, this was the only thing she was hungry for.

Not everyone was shopping or working. The doors of tea rooms and chop houses began to open around the edge of the market, despite the early hour. There were food stalls, tray sellers and all manner of cooking smells along with the scents of ale and cider, beer and gin. Plenty of opportunity to eat, drink and be merry.

Everywhere, there was magic — sparks of growth and protection, shops and stalls overspilling with glass-bottled philtres, and magicians doing tricks of transformation and bewitchment to draw small penny crowds around them. No metallurmages, Flavia noted, but the day was still young.

She hadn't worked out Ygraine's magic, yet. She knew the young princess must have some — she'd mentioned proximity sparks, after all, and that wasn't a trick for novices. But there was nothing of the confident enchantress about her, either.

Carriages and carts arrived every minute, pouring out customers and tourists ready to see the sights and spend their coin. The market unfurled like a bright summer flower, waking up brighter and louder as more people arrived.

"How are we going to find one drunken alchemist in all this crush?" Flavia asked.

Orlando shrugged, not looking especially bothered. "We'll get lucky."

"I'm so glad you have a plan."

Orlando was in his element here. He swapped cheerful pleasantries with stallholders even as his eyes flicked here and there, observing everything. He was like a cat on the prowl, or an impresario at the stage door. Flower sellers greeted him as an old friend with kisses and smiles, pleased to answer any question he put to them.

"Nothing touches him, does it?" Ygraine murmured in Flavia's ear. "He breezes through the world, causing chaos and mayhem wherever he walks, and never has to suffer the consequences."

Flavia gave her an impatient look. "If you dislike him so much, why are you still here?"

Ygraine's cheeks flared red with anger. "You speak to me as if I were..."

"You can't have it both ways," Flavia retorted. If Ygraine was going to behave like a child, then she knew how to manage children. "If you wanted to be treated like a princess, you should never have set foot outside Buckingham Palace."

Ygraine looked outraged for a second, then glanced away, avoiding her eyes. "You're right. I can't afford airs and graces right now." She took a deep, heavy breath. "I don't trust him," she said quietly. "That's what it comes down to. I've known the Device brothers for more than a decade, since my machine-mad uncle dragged them into the royal household. Rinaldo has a good heart, but Orlando doesn't have a heart at all. I loved him once. He was a dear friend and companion, but now? I don't trust him an inch, and neither should you."

Princess Ygraine pressed her lips closed after that, to stop any further words from lashing out in the open air.

Flavia was bemused by this unhappy character reference. It didn't fit with what she knew about the Device brothers, not at all. "You can trust him in this," she promised. "He wants to rescue Rinaldo and your husband so badly. He'll stop at nothing."

"Oh, Rinaldo!" Ygraine grumbled. "Don't talk to me about Rinaldo. There is *nothing* he won't do for that brother of his, and to the devil with the rest of us!"

"Rinaldo is lost," Flavia said, grating the words out between her teeth. "He is in the most dangerous place I can possibly imagine, and my children are there with him. I trust Orlando to get them back. You might try it."

Ygraine was unimpressed with her fervour. "You're in love with one or other of them, I suppose. You wouldn't be the first."

"Your world is very small if that is all you can imagine," Flavia shot back.

There was a scuffle ahead of them in the crowd, followed by panicked shouting. Flavia only realised that she had lost sight of Orlando when he burst back through the crush of people, one arm locked around the neck of a small, bearded tray-seller in a shabby suit. The tray hung around his neck on straps of leather, and the man had to struggle to prevent his wares (various glass bottles with wax stoppers) from smashing on the cobblestones.

"Look what I found!" Orlando declared with a delighted roar. "Mr Ignatious Cavendish, the finest alchemist who can be bought for tuppence! Lucky, eh?"

Flavia shot an amused glance at Ygraine, who huffed a reluctant smile. If they had to rely on luck, at least Orlando wasn't short of it.

What could have happened between the Device brothers and Princess Ygraine? Flavia had no trouble believing that it was a great inconvenience to have your husband transformed into a clockwork cat on your wedding day, but there was something else going on here, something deeper. A friendship that had gone badly awry.

What was she missing?

~

Orlando was not dead. Of course Orlando was not dead, because this was not Orlando. Rinaldo had barely pressed hands to his brother's chest before the creature started laughing at him. His brother's face fell away to show a mask of pink blossom and spiny rose twigs: laughing eyes, a cruel and mocking mouth.

"Not much of a joke," Rinaldo said roughly, trying to calm his rapid pulse.

"That depends on where you're sitting," teased the not-Orlando. His shirt fell away to display a bare chest the colour of autumn leaves even as his body shrank to a quarter of his size. He wore a few garlands of matching blossom which barely counted as clothes.

"Have you seen my cat?" Rinaldo asked.

The fairy giggled. "Why of all things green and good should I want to help you? Your face is bare and you're not nearly as pretty as I am."

Rinaldo felt ridiculous for even suggesting this, but he was feeling lost and it wasn't like it mattered to him either way. "If kisses are currency..." he said awkwardly.

The fairy laughed again, long and loud in trills of delight. "Kisses aren't to be handed out like flower stems at a moonlight dance, dear thing. The only kiss worth having is the one that is *stolen*."

"So, what do I do?" Rinaldo asked impatiently. "What would it take to get you to help me?"

"I don't know," said the fairy. "I've never wanted anything." He rose up quickly in the air with a burr of *wings*, actual wings that looked like something belonging to a bee. "I'll let you know if I get inspired!" He swished away in a blur of light and giggles, leaving Rinaldo alone by the river.

Nothing to do but walk.

The Daedalus Club was not the grandest or most palatial of the gentleman's clubs in Pall Mall, but there was a scientific dignity to its half-dozen marble columns. Flavia was not surprised in the least when the footman who greeted them in the lobby expressed silent dismay at the appearance of herself and Ygraine, and promptly sent for the day manager.

This gentleman, who looked as much like a butler as any fellow that Flavia had ever known before, wore a crisp suit matched to a crisp expression, as if the

footman had ironed his entire self along with that day's
newspapers.

"Mr Device," said the day manager, his voice
vibrating with gentle disapproval. "You are as welcome
here as any valued member of this establishment. But
ladies cannot be admitted on any day other than the
twenty-third of the month, unless it has been declared
a special visiting day. Not even if the Empress of India
herself chose to grace us with her presence."

Ygraine let out a tiny snort.

The manager was devoting all of his attention to
not looking directly at the ladies who had crossed his
threshold uninvited, and thus had failed to realise he
was in the presence of royalty; either that, or he was a
master of ignoring any reality that did not conform to
the rules of the Daedalus Club.

When it came to Mr Cavendish, who still had his
philtre tray around his neck and was the shabbiest of
the four of them, the manager merely allowed himself a
sniff of disdain. "Mr Device is of course allowed to
bring guests of the masculine persuasion at any time,
providing they behave in a gentlemanly manner," he
said, his tone suggesting that if he could find any justifi-
cation to throw Mr Cavendish out on his ear, he would
do so with the strength of thousands.

Considering the distressing smell coming from the
alchemist, Flavia was not surprised.

Orlando glanced at Ygraine, Cavendish and Flavia
and managed somehow to put the blankest possible

expression upon his pretty face. Then he smiled, and it was as if every lamp in the building flared suddenly to life. "I don't know what you're talking about, Mr Jenkins," he said. "These three chaps are my assistants and I assure you there's nothing womanly about any of them. We need a few hours in the South Laboratory, and I promise we'll leave by the side door afterwards."

There was a long, agonising pause. Mr Jenkins allowed his disapproving gaze to pass briefly over Cavendish's tray, Ygraine's midnight silk opera cloak, and Flavia's... well, whatever he noticed about Flavia. A tired expression and a shape too tightly corseted to ever be mistaken for male, she rather expected.

"For science, Jenkins," Orlando added, with weight to his words.

"Very well, Mr Device," said the manager finally. "For science."

R inaldo followed the river northwards, keeping his eyes on the sun. After what felt like hours, he finally realised that the sun never moved, or if it did it was in no predictable manner. He had no chance of learning which direction was north.

It was cooler in this part of the greenwood, more of a Britannian climate with the smell of autumn and acorns in the air instead of a lush, endless summer.

Up ahead, through the trees, Rinaldo saw flickers

of unusual light; reflections off something that might be silver, or chrome, or nothing at all. He shouldn't trust it. There were entire ballads about how the primary function of fairies was tricking mortals into getting lost, and while Rinaldo might not have actually read many of them, he was aware of the conventions of the genre.

Don't follow fairies into a forest. When stuck in Faerie, anything you follow into a forest is probably also a fairy. Unless it's a cat.

Still, he was achieving nothing useful wandering along a river on his own. If there was even half a chance of him finding metal in this world of botanical magic, it was worth the risk.

When Rinaldo plunged into the forest, he did indeed find fairies, but not one of them was likely to steal a kiss. Instead, he found six figures caught in a circle, frozen in the act of dancing. They were all human-sized, more or less, with long limbs, and hair that spun out like the spray of water from a fountain, or fronds from a weeping willow tree.

Statues. Impossible statues, captured in such a moment of life with their masked faces tossed this way and that, their wings in mid-flutter, their feet kicked into the air.

It was as if someone had cut them from paper, hung them from ribbons. But they were real. Solid. Weren't they?

Rinaldo reached out a tentative hand to one of the creatures. His hand came into contact with a warm

cheek, feeling the rough edge of a mask made from scal-
loped leaves. These fairies were alive. Had someone
cast a spell on them? Perhaps this was how they slept.

A gleam of light caught his eye further on through
the trees and he followed it.

Here, Rinaldo found another living statue, so to
speak. The hands, unmarked by labour, lay intact and
separate on the grass. Someone had smashed the arms,
torso and head into tiny pieces.

There was no blood.

The legs were broken more deliberately into
segments barely a hand-span thick. They were laid out
on the grass to recreate the shape of a body. Even if this
were a statue and not the remains of a person, it would
make a gruesome and chilling sight.

Why would a fairy to this to one of their own kind?

There was a rustle in the trees nearby. Rinaldo
whipped his head around just in time to see a wild-
eyed fellow lurch up out of the trees, his spectacles all
but falling off his nose.

Not fairy. Human.

"You!" Rinaldo exclaimed.

This was the man whose body had been stolen by
the fairy Quicksilver. Murderer and thief, wrapped in
the skin of an Earl's son. The Honourable Perrault
Gloucester.

There was little of the murderer about this man
now. He still wore his fine suit, though it had seen
better days — Mrs Hopkins from the orphanage would

have rolled out one of her favourite phrases here: he looked like he had been dragged through a hedge backwards.

Mr Gloucester turned on Rinaldo with desperation in his eyes, hands grasping at the other man's lapels. "Did you find her? Do you know where she is?" He looked drunk or concussed, and not only because of the disgraceful state of his shirtfront. His eyes were half glazed over with shock or terror. "She was here, and now — she could be in anyone." The poor man leaped back suddenly, twitching as if he were afraid of touching Rinaldo. "Is it you? Is she in you?"

"Who are we talking about?" Rinaldo asked.

"The monster," hissed Mr Gloucester and then turned and ran, crashing through the trees.

Rinaldo heard a tiny sound behind him, like a child clearing its throat. He turned warily and saw a barefoot young boy in pyjamas standing near him in the thicket.

"I rather think he's talking about me," said Master Dashmond Gloucester. His eyes glowed silver.

Ygraine

sister of Princess Evanna, Countess of Orkney

Evanna's death was more mundane than the others. Her husband the Earl of Orkney had no time for love philtres, and I never heard their lives were ever touched by magic.

Evanna had four children: all sons. She performed spectacularly as the wife and mother she was supposed to be, and created the next generation of Isoldan heirs.

Gawain, Agravaine, Gaheris, Gareth.

Four babies in six years, and the last one killed her. Love philtres aren't the only blight on our world.

The gentlemen's club: an institution that persists today, though it enjoyed its greatest social peak during the Isoldan Empire. Was it the powerful, steel-corseted figure of Queen Isolda who sent so many gentlemen scurrying to these bastions of masculinity? Every club, from the pre-eminent White's to the fictional Diogenes of Sherlock Holmes fame, had a particular tone based on what type of gentleman was allowed to take membership.

In the scientific clubs and magical societies, the institutions became something else: not merely a communal haven for dining in male company, but an entire world in which one's chosen intellectual pursuit determined one's peers. Some of the greatest marvels of the day were first dreamed up over port and cigars with fellow members of the Spenser, the Da Vinci, or the Daedalus.

— Bertram MacNee, *Masculinity & Magic*, 1983

Chapter 5

In Which One Should be Suspicious of Both Cakes and Tea

The laboratory on the fourth floor of the Daedalus Club was magnificent: a wide and airy room with excellent natural light streaming in from the windows, and plenty of lamps for the twenty hours of the day when there was no daylight to be had. Long tables, gleaming glass vessels, and all manner of arcane equipment were set out for the usage of members only.

Every spare surface was wood-panelled or covered in smooth marble. There were glass shelves along the back of the room, containing all manner of odd ingredients and other fascinating curios such as a mummified hand and what might be a prehistoric tooth.

Queenie would be delighted by this place, Flavia considered. And she would throw a fit as soon as she realised membership was exclusive to men...

"There are six laboratories in the building, plus a basement workshop or three," said Orlando, looking proud. "Membership of the Daedalus is one of the best things your family's patronage ever got me, your —" He paused, glancing at Cavendish and then at the princess. "Yorlanda," he finished, creating a pseudonym with surprising deftness.

"I'm so glad it was useful to you, Borlando," Ygraine replied with an acid smile.

Cavendish barely seemed aware of Ygraine, or Flavia come to that. Still clutching the tray around his neck as if afraid it was going to be snatched from him, he moved around the laboratory, peering at everything. "Splendid, very splendid, indeed yes," he muttered. "Get a man a drink, Device?"

Orlando smiled broadly. "You'll get a drink when you're finished, Cavendish."

"Can't work without a drink."

"You don't know what work I have in mind." Orlando pulled out his little leather-wrapped bundle from inside the coat he had stolen from Actaeon Place earlier that day. Carefully, he unwrapped it to reveal a series of little brass beetles. "Believe me, we won't want to risk contamination."

Cavendish snorted, and wiped his nose on his hand. "Yah, what's so special about them?"

"These contain samples of water from every enchanted fountain in the legendary Forest of Arden," said Orlando. "A cornucopia of powerful, priceless philtres, from love and hate to wisdom, transformation and... the water of worlds." His eyes briefly met Flavia's, which widened as she realised what it was he intended to do. "I need you to figure out which is which."

Cavendish looked unimpressed. "Why don't yon taste them t'find out?"

"Because oblivion is one of the options! I also don't fancy falling madly in hate with anyone in this room, do you? Can you do this, or do I need to dredge up one of the *other* great alchemists who owes me for keeping him out of debtor's prison?"

Cavendish snorted again, and finally took the tray from around his neck, setting it on a side bench. "And you've a good reason for not labelling the little critters with aforethought, have you?"

Flavia had been about to ask the same thing; Queenie would not have approved of this half-baked method.

One of the brass beetles began to slowly walk away on little legs. Orlando caught it between finger and thumb, deactivating it with some kind of secret switch. "These aren't exactly my best work," he said with an embarrassed smile. "I used the good set for the enchantress who was blackmailing me and holding my... friend hostage."

"Friend?" Ygraine said sharply.

"Cat," Flavia translated.

"I see." If possible, her tone sharpened further. "Orlando, I remember these metal bugs of yours. You used to use them to add sugar to tea a decade ago, and they were hit-or-miss then."

"They're excellent at holding liquids without breaking!" Orlando insisted. "Unfortunately, I had them in my pocket at a suffragette rally a few years ago, and they got it into their head to be rebellious. I haven't been able to get them to follow orders ever since — and they *hate* to be labelled."

~

H ours passed. There was little for Flavia or Ygraine to do. Cavendish worked on testing the philtres, and Orlando hovered around him, anxious for any positive result. Twice now, Orlando had forcibly scrubbed Cavendish's hands after a possible contamination, only for the alchemist to spill even more on the table the second Orlando's back was turned.

"He's not used to being the responsible brother," Ygraine observed, swinging her feet as she sat on the bench nearest the window. "It's almost amusing — or it would be if I wasn't still furious with him." She fidgeted a little, twitching at the cloak. It was remarkably warm in here — some form of ingenious heating system that kept the floors quite toasty. Having a membership made up of rogue scientists was clearly paying off for the Daedalus Club.

"You can remove it, you know," Flavia suggested. "Unless you do only have your night-things underneath?"

Ygraine gave her a haughty glare — the princess seemed largely made of haughty glares — and shrugged off her billowy layer of silk. The gown beneath was excellently and expensively tailored. There was no bustle in sight — only a few months ago, in her previous job for the Earnsley family, Flavia had been dragged around a series of modistes to help her former charges build a trousseau for their European finishing school. The girls had resisted any attempt to add yardage in the back end. "It's all about princess-cut these days," the girls wailed. "No one wants a bustle any more!"

This, Flavia knew, was the princess in question. Ygraine wore the fashion she had popularised in recent years: dark colours, trim-waisted gowns with high collars, and layers of fabric flowing from the knee to the floor instead of being bunched up around the figure. She looked too rich to be real, like an illustration on a chocolate box.

Always dark colours, never bright. The palace was always in at least half-mourning, thanks to the bad luck that had been cast upon the royal family. The Earnsley daughters had adored royal gossip almost as much as Flavia's great aunt, and she felt as if she knew every fact about the princesses that had ever appeared in the newspapers.

That didn't mean she knew the real Princess Ygraine: the angry young lady who had followed them all the way from Buckingham Palace in an opera cloak.

"Will there be trouble if you don't go back?" Flavia said, in as neutral a voice as she could manage. She had no wish to pick a fight with the princess, but she couldn't help thinking of how easily she and Orlando might disappear into a prison if frantic palace guards decided they were kidnappers.

"Perhaps," muttered Ygraine. "I just couldn't bear it any longer."

"Since the wedding?" Flavia asked. Not that she was wildly curious, of course, but she still did not know nearly enough about what the Device brothers had done, to get themselves declared public enemies.

Ygraine gave a cynical laugh. "Oh yes," she said. "The wedding. Because everything was so perfect before that."

A whoop of delight went up from Orlando. "Water of wisdom for anyone?" He waved a glass vial (properly labelled) in triumph, then handed it back to Mr Cavendish. "My good sir, would it be out of the question for you to swallow a drop or two of this before proceeding with the work?"

Mr Cavendish blew the contents of his nose into a handkerchief so grubby that it was surely worthy of having its own scientific experiments performed on it.

"Took a swig ten minutes ago," he grunted. "See me fly now, m'boy!"

Orlando clapped his hands.

Princess Ygraine stared out of the window and looked grim.

Flavia wondered if it would be possible to get a cup of tea anytime soon. Failing that, a nap?

She left the princess's side and had a wander around the laboratory. Not for the first time, she wished Queenie was here. If anyone deserved a chance to label magical philtres while hopped up on the Water of Wisdom, it was her earnest young charge.

Flavia opened one door and found a cupboard of scientific instruments and vessels. All most dull. A second side door led her to a tiny drawing room with barely half a window lighting it. It did feature a reading couch and a small library of journals and periodicals.

The reading couch was more than sufficient to her needs. Flavia went to fetch her stolen coat and settled herself down for a quick rest.

For the first time in months, she dreamed of Faerie.

F laxenseed knew this place. The bend of the trees, the warm scent of the flowers, and the crisp crunch of autumn leaves underfoot was all so familiar. She had danced here, so many times, caught up in the music and the masks and the kissing and the freedom of her mother's country.

There was no dancing now. Flavia could see the remains of a feast, spilled out across tree trunk tables, but the honey cakes were stale and the fruit was over-ripe, spoiling where it sat. No one had been here in a long while.

What had happened to Faerie? Had they already crossed over to the mortal world, leaving all of this behind?

Flavia stumbled on. It was common in these dreams of hers to feel no hunger or tiredness; she could touch, but was never truly alive in Faerie. All her life she had wanted nothing more than to be here for real, to taste the fruit and honey.

Now she felt an awful impatience. How had she thought this world so splendid, when it would happily sacrifice children?

(If it was so wonderful, why were the fairies so hungry to escape?)

Flavia came over the crest of the hill, searching for her mother's open bower, all blossom and fern, set above the wide dancing field. Flavia had loved that bower, often curling up at the feet of her beautiful queen, lapping up every word that fell from her mouth.

Oh, mother. Please don't hate me.

This time, in place of the bower, what she saw was a house.

It was an odd and elaborate construction. Apple branches, trailing willow weeps, brambles and creeping vines had all been woven together in a pattern that was utterly haphazard and yet... familiar.

I know that house.

There were the front steps, and the walls with magnolia clusters as window panes.

Her mother had always slept in the open air, where she could see and feel everyone. What had happened to Tanaquil Gloriana that she needed such walls around her? This was practically a castle with draw-bridge, keeping the rest of Faerie at bay.

There was no life here, no birdsong or music. There was only the house, grim and magnificent and awful.

These steps should not have held her weight, formed as they were from thin tangles of jasmine and fresh hawthorn. When Flavia stepped on them, they crunched like autumn leaves underfoot, but nothing broke. The house held her up, step by step, until she stood in the entrance hall.

The familiarity made sense now. This was not just a house. It was Gloucester Worth and Number 12 Actaeon Place, rolled into one. Smaller in scale, perhaps, but the arrangement of the rooms and ceilings was that of a proper Britannian manor.

Where on earth had Tanaquil Gloriana found a competent architect when her court had the attention span of squirrels?

Flavia wanted to run from room to room, to discover everything about this bizarre house of tree-and-branch, but she could not countenance climbing higher into the construction. What if the floor melted away beneath her feet? She knew from long experience that she could be hurt in dreams.

Quicksilver had hurt her once. An accident, it seemed at the time — knocking Flavia from a tree branch from sheer carelessness. It had made Flavia less inclined to trust her, after that. She was proved horribly right years later, when she saw the blood of Mrs Brundage the cook on the hands of her former lover and friend.

Flavia decided to investigate the kitchens of the tree-and-branch house. How far would the comparison hold? Did this house have foundations? Would there be men made of straw and leaves chained up the cellar, for true authenticity?

The kitchens were darker than the other rooms, partially underground with little sunlight coming in from the rooms above. Here, Flavia found the first person she had seen alive in Faerie since this dream began.

Queenie Gloucester.

The girl sat tall and straight at a table woven of thin grasses and walnut twigs. Her hair was wild, with enough twigs and other nesting supplies to delight your average robin. To Flavia's horror, the girl was eating a cake. Powdered sugar and cream clung to her fingers.

"Miss Wednesday!" Queenie said in surprise, looking up as her governess entered the makeshift kitchen of moss walls and sturdy tree branches. "Is that you? You seem quite insubstantial."

"Ever the scientist," said Flavia. "I'm here in my dreams."

Queenie gave her a sharp look, licking her fingers. "You can't rescue us, then?"

"Not yet. Orlando Device has a plan."

"Saints be praised, Orlando Device has a plan!" the girl said, every bit as cynical as the Princess Ygraine. She followed Flavia's gaze to the near-empty plate of cakes before her. "I was hungry," she said defensively. "This is practically my home. Why should I not eat cakes?"

"You've never paid much attention to fairy stories, have you?" Flavia sighed.

"Fairy stories are for children," said the young alchemist. "I prefer facts. Do you know where my brother is?"

"I'm sure he'll turn up, especially if there are cream cakes on offer." Flavia was worried about that cake. There were too many fairy ballads that made it clear eating and drinking were a trap for mortals. "Have you seen a yellow cat?" she asked. "Or any of the others who came through when you did?"

"Aunt Elspeth's around," Queenie shrugged. "I was with Rinaldo for a while but he got lost in the forest. Or I did. It's hard to be sure what is true around here, so many comings and goings. I haven't seen any fairies at all, though I'm sure they wouldn't add much to my scientific understanding of the world." She frowned at the remains of the cream cake that she still held between her fingers. "Why does this taste of acorns?"

"I think perhaps," said Flavia. "You should get out of here right now."

She led the girl up to the ground level, through the entry hall and out to the front steps, but the moment Flavia felt real grass beneath her feet again, she turned to see Queenie standing back in the middle of the entry hall.

"Come here," Flavia ordered, using her sternest governess voice.

"I don't think I can," said Queenie. She had a troubled expression on her face. "I think, Miss Wednesday, that I should not have eaten those cakes." She crumpled a little, as if about to swoon.

Flavia ran back to her, but the door slammed hard in her face, all oak branches bedecked with bluebells. "Queenie, I'll come back for you!" she shouted through the door. "Wait here. Stay safe."

"Send books and tea!" the girl called wanly through the cracks in the door.

Flavia startled awake in total darkness and lay there blinking for a long moment. Why would her mother create a floral replica of the two grand houses belonging to the Gloucester family?

Where were all the fairies?

She returned to the laboratory. Lamps were burning here. Mr Cavendish worked away, surrounded by test tubes and beakers. It was night. A whole day and evening had passed.

Orlando and Ygraine sat together on a high bench near the darkened window, talking in low voices. Neither looked happy. The staff of the Daedalus Club had overcome their concerns about female visitors long enough to serve tea, though neither Orlando or Ygraine drank — they toyed with cups and saucers and sugar tongs, anything to avoid each other's gaze.

Flavia stopped in the doorway, not alerting them to her presence. Had there had been some love affair there, or some other romantic complication? It might explain Ygraine's venomous attitude towards the Device brothers.

Or was she just as close-minded as the princess, to assume that was the reason?

Orlando finished arranging a cup of tea to his liking and placed it back on the tray. "It wasn't deliberate, you know. None of it. We only ever meant the best for you."

"I didn't know," Ygraine said softly. "Why you were so set on preventing me from taking that philtre."

"It's a beastly practice," Orlando huffed. "Bad enough you had to marry someone you barely know — but taking a philtre to become eternally besotted?"

Ygraine put the sugar tongs back in the bowl with some force. "How else is a princess to experience love?"

"It's not love, believe me," he growled. "I've been dosed with love philtres a dozen times or more, and it's not anything like the real thing."

The princess arched an eyebrow at him. "The great Orlando Device and his many seductions. How do you know it's not good enough? To what are you comparing the experience?"

He gave her a furious look, which she met quite calmly.

"It's a fair question," she added.

"I know," he muttered. "But Ygraine, with your family history, your sisters, how can you..."

"I don't want to talk about my sisters." Ygraine raised her cup near her lips and sighed. "I thought you wrecked my wedding because of Rinaldo. You and your dreadful matchmaking imperative."

Orlando laughed out loud; a bitter sound. "He's made it very clear to me that I was wrong."

"I'm astounded that he needed to do so!"

"I thought... maybe you liked each other a little. It would have made sense of why you were always

103

huddling in corners together. You were angry at him these last few years, and I never knew why."

"Now I'm angry at both of you," she sighed. "How exhausting."

"If you'd taken the philtre, you wouldn't have been yourself any more," said Orlando. "Three of your sisters *died* because of love philtres, Ygraine."

"They were compelled to love men other than their husbands," Ygraine retorted. "That awful Tristan, who destroyed Iseult. If she'd drunk her husband's philtre as Arwenna did, as I was going to, she would still be alive."

"Arwenna," Orlando said flatly. "Your surviving sister. Tell me, when did she last smile at you while her husband was in the room? When did she last speak a word of kindness to your mother?"

Ygraine stared at him, confusion still reigning over her freckled face. "No one was forcing me, Orlando."

"Have you seen the wives who take the philtre? They become jealous wrecks, or they smile into the tea trolley while their husband dallies with the maids. They never argue with their husbands over dinner. What the hell sort of man would marry you and not want to argue with you every day of the week?"

"Don't talk like that," Ygraine begged. "You sound like —"

"Who?"

She stared at her lap, looking just a little heartbroken. "Someone I used to know."

"Your mother didn't take a philtre," Orlando said flatly. "And she rules an Empire. She conquered whole continents because she didn't die of grief when she became a widow. Arwenna's husband is twenty years older than her. What do you think is going to happen to your sister when her husband dies?"

To fill the silence that followed, Ygraine snatched up her teacup and drank down the contents. A moment later, her eyes rolled up into her head and she fell into a dead faint on the floor. The china cup shattered at her feet.

Ygraine

and her Majesty's Royal Engineers

The map was my idea. "If you really want to keep living here in the palace and using Uncle Albert's workshop," I told the boys. "You had better find a way to show Mama it's worth keeping you."

"We don't need your mother," Orlando said stubbornly. He kept insisting he and Rinaldo could take to the road as travelling performers any time they liked — royal patronage could go hang.

Rinaldo looked sick at the thought of becoming an itinerant magician. I didn't blame him. Buckingham Palace was my prison, but I wasn't naive enough to think that living outside of it would be easy.

Representatives came almost daily now, bringing elaborate gifts to please Mama: from the distant colonies, and the European countries under her sway. A month ago, she had been presented with a new map of India, which marked every conquered Britannian territory in a bright purple ink. It was already out of date. "Surely you can top that," I suggested.

Orlando's eyes lit up at the challenge. He began to tease his brother about his childhood obsession of poring over atlases and learning place names.

I left them to it.

Three days later, I was summoned to a rare tea with Mama, at which the Device brothers revealed their gift for her: a table of bronze depicting the Britannian Empire in all its glory. Magic was soldered into its metal heart, so the continents shifted and changed colour to acknowledge new countries and territories when they were beaten by our forces.

The air smelled of sulphur and sparks: both boys looked exhausted, but proud.

"My Royal Engineers," said Queen Isolda with a smile warmer than I had seen her wear on any of her daughters' wedding days. "What a prize you are."

"At your Majesty's service," replied Orlando Device, bowing low.

That was the beginning of it all. The Miraculous and Extraordinary Device Brothers. Within a year they were all velvet suits and top hats, rolled out at every function to demonstrate their miracles. Darlings of the court.

I'm not sure Orlando remembered for a second that it was my idea. I know for a fact that Mama has always believed it was hers.

Rinaldo, at least, was warmer to me afterwards. At least one of them knew how to be grateful.

I spent time in the workshop again. It still smelled like Papa, all steam and metal, and I liked to poke at whatever new project the sparks were playing with.

My governesses told me this interest was unbecoming for a princess. I smiled and simpered and practiced my Frankish verbs like a good girl and still returned to the workshop whenever I liked. Who was going to stop me?

Orlando and Rinaldo had their own tutors to worry about! Elocution lessons, languages, and a smattering of politics and geography — enough to be useful, and to direct their inventions towards Mama's best interests.

I was offended when I realised their education was to be more extensive than mine — but then I started to sit in on their classes, daring the tutor to report me.

Dance classes were far more entertaining now Orlando and Rinaldo had been ordered to attend. Mama insisted that her royal engineers should learn the life of the court, so that their marvels could be displayed with honour and professional dignity.

"She's trying to turn you both into princesses," I teased Orlando as we practiced the Austrian waltz together.

"There are worse fates," mused Orlando as he twirled me.

When it came to dance partners, Rinaldo was awkward and stoic, going through the moves like an automaton recalling every inch of the blueprints.

Orlando might tread on my feet on occasion, but at least he danced like he wanted to be there.

～

When I turned sixteen, the murmurs about my future grew louder: the last marriage to be arranged. As yet, there was no formal betrothal on the books.

Mama was not aware of my regular visits to the workshop, nor that many of my visits were with Orlando, unchaperoned. No one worried about that sort of thing when we were children and somehow, they had fallen into the habit of not thinking about it now that I was in full corsets.

She commissioned the Device Brothers to make me a jewellery tree for my birthday, and deliberately misunderstood the assignment, creating an enormous bronze tree with enough branches to hold the Crown Jewels.

Not long after that, Rinaldo became distracted by a new Royal project. Mama had imported a team of experts to build an authentic Indian garden in the west corner of the gardens. Rinaldo offered to assist with the construction of an automated watering system, as well as a magical dome to reconstruct the warmer weather patterns that were necessary for banyan, eucalyptus and mango trees to thrive.

Orlando sulked over the project for no reason I understood, and I often found him alone in the workshop while Rinaldo was busy.

It was fun at first, to have Orlando to myself without his cautious shadow. I loved hearing him rattling on about all his nonsensical theories while he tinkered with this and that, bringing his miracles to life.

As the Indian garden project dragged on, Rinaldo chose to spend more and more time outside the palace, inhaling the stories that Mr Ambedkar and the other gardeners could tell him about their lives back home in Ceylon, or Burma. Orlando's smile became brighter and more brittle.

One morning, I approached the workshop on silent stockinged feet. I could already hear angry shouts from several corridors away.

"Why shouldn't I learn about my country?" Rinaldo growled.

"Why do you even care?" Orlando flung at him. "You've never been there, it's not *yours*. You come from an orphanage in Bath."

"I want something that's mine," Rinaldo said, and there was an almost painful note of longing in his voice. "We don't all have fairy tales about theatre troupes and silk blankets to fall back on."

"You have me. We have our work, and the Queen

will give us fame and fortune as long as we make marvels for her. Why can't you be happy with our dreams coming true?" Orlando sounded ragged, exhausted.

I had noticed his lack of energy lately and put it down to his being in a state of jealousy. Perhaps there was something else?

"I don't have anything," growled Rinaldo. "This royal pantomime isn't going to last. Sooner or later they'll cast us out, and when it all falls to dust, what will I have left?"

I had never heard either of them sound so miserable before, so lost.

"I'm not going to leave you!" Orlando shouted at his brother. "I'm not going anywhere."

There was a scuffling sound. Rinaldo's next words were muffled but it sounded a lot like: "That's what Mr Albert said."

What? I shoved the workshop door open, caught in a wash of heat. As always, it was the hottest place in the palace — with the possible exception now of the Indian garden, which was humid enough to make my hair curl. "*What* did you say about my uncle?"

They were so tall now, both of them, tall enough that anyone in the street would call them men, not boys. The brothers stared wildly at me, caught in the act of shoving at each other. Orlando's shirt was rucked open, and for a moment I saw a flash of dark red against his skin before he tugged the shirt back, making himself respectable. "Nothing," he muttered.

Rinaldo stared at the floor.

"Uncle Albert died of his stomach complaint," I said, my voice sounding too loud in the echoing workshop. "Didn't he?"

The boys stared at the floor, and at the walls, and anywhere except each other.

"You oughtn't keep secrets from me," I said crossly.

Orlando and Rinaldo refused to speak to me until I dropped the subject.

Many nineteenth century authors address class prejudice, but Gaskell and Bronte both do so with particular reference to magic, and the social norms surrounding the usage of philtres, sparks and charms across the different social spheres of Isoldan Britannia: Jane Eyre is unprepared for the love philtre offered to her by Rochester because she does not come from a class in which young ladies are trained from birth to avoid such dangers; the ladies of Cranford gossip constantly about the enchantments used by those of their acquaintance, but are shocked to hear of similar usage among the underclasses.

— Mildred Hode, "Everyday Magic and Power in Isoldan Novels (by Female Authors)," *Atheniad* Vol. 12 (1972)

Chapter 6

In Which Philtres Do Not Belong in Teacups

Orlando threw himself on the floor next to the crumpled figure of Ygraine. "Cavendish!" he shouted through the doorway. "What the hellfire did you do?"

"The tests were going too slowly," called back the alchemist, from where he pottered at the bench. "I was almost certain this vial contained the Water of Truth."

"Her cup, you bastard! What was in the princess's cup?"

"Not Truth, apparently." Cavendish had the gall to sound annoyed by that.

"Death," guessed Flavia, coming to Orlando's side as he turned Ygraine gently on to her back. "Look at her."

The princess's breathing was shallow. When Flavia brushed fingertips against her cheek, her skin was cold to the touch.

Orlando stared in horror as her limp body. "CAVENDISH! Tell me you've isolated the Water of Undoing."

"Well, of course," said the alchemist in a huffy voice. "You don't think I'd perform live experiments without having the Water of Undoing to hand, do you?"

"I'm not making any assumptions about your ethics at this point, man!"

Flavia hurried to Cavendish's side and snatched the beaker from him. "Are you certain this is the one?"

"Oh yes," said the alchemist certainly. "No, wait, it's this one." At the last moment, he swapped it for another beaker.

She made a frustrated sound. "May I suggest you label them?" *Politeness*, she reminded herself. There was nothing to be gained by bellowing like Orlando. She had learned long ago that if a woman needed something from a man, politeness was the only option. Only men with wealth — and occasionally, their wives — had the option to shout their demands into the air. It was difficult to remain calm and civil when she wanted to start strangling alchemists with her gloved hands until there were none left in the world, but she had been practicing politeness her whole life.

"It's all up here," Cavendish assured her with a gap-toothed smile, tapping his own skull.

"It's going to be thrown out the window in a

minute, you bounder," snarled Orlando. "We're losing her."

Flavia splashed drops from the beaker into Ygraine's mouth. The princess' lips were bright red, her skin bone white, like something out of a fairy tale. "How much does she need?"

"A drop should do it," said Orlando, staring down at the unmoving girl. He lurched to his feet, strode back and forth. "Blast it."

Ygraine gasped, and her eyelashes fluttered. "That tea tastes terrible," she groaned.

"Damnations of the Empire," breathed Orlando. Her recovery meant that his anger had nowhere to go. He stood up and stormed out of the room, his boots echoing away down the corridor.

There was a tiny wrinkle above Ygraine's nose that mostly appeared when Orlando did something objectionable. As far as Flavia was concerned, it might as well be her default facial expression. "What's crawled up his britches?" sighed the princess.

"It's an alchemy thing," Flavia said, not knowing how to break it to the princess that she had nearly died — perhaps had actually died, for a moment or two. "You know how it is with scientists. Differences of opinion." Carefully, she helped Ygraine into the most comfortable chair in the room, not wanting to risk the bench. "Do you feel quite well?"

"I didn't swoon, did I? How embarrassing." Ygraine plucked helplessly at her dress. "I told my maid this corset was too tight, but we were in such a rush." She glanced around in alarm as if realising she had mentioned corsets in a room where men was present, but Cavendish had already turned back to his work.

"Sit for a moment," Flavia urged.

She knelt at Ygraine's feet, hiding her face discreetly until she could be sure her own breathing had returned to normal. She then stood up, walked briskly over to Cavendish the Alchemist and spoke to him very firmly in her governess voice until he grudgingly labelled all of the philtres so far identified. Once this task was completed to her satisfaction, and only then, did Flavia go in search of Orlando Device.

"I rather think he's talking about me," said Master Dashmond Gloucester in a sweet, but chilling voice. "You're the professor, aren't you? The one who made the pretty fountain out of bronze. Such a shame you had to destroy it." He did not sound like a child, which was the first sign that something was terribly wrong.

Rinaldo had only met Dashmond twice, first at the fair and then in the Forest of Arden. There had been a bright cheekiness about the boy, even when he was half asleep. Now there was a cold, silver light in his eyes. His hair was slick, far too tidy for any regular child.

He had made himself a mask of ivy. The fronds

trailed dirt-strewn roots across the boy's collarbone. No, not a boy.

Rinaldo was starting to be able to spot the signs of a fairy pretending to be human. This one had gone further than most — the body was clearly flesh and blood.

"You are the monster, then?" Rinaldo asked, for something to say as he calculated whether or not this fairy-stolen child was a danger to him.

Dashmond blinked with wide, innocent eyes. "My queen thought so. *I'm* quite insulted."

Rinaldo stepped out of the way as the boy came forward, but it was the broken body on the grass that was of interest rather than Rinaldo himself. The boy circled the smashed shape, peering here and there, dislodging a particularly large lump of leg with his toe.

"She stopped trusting me," he said with a tragic air. "Though I did it all for her. I promised her all the worlds, polished and poached on a platter. Is your queen as cruel as mine?"

Rinaldo was startled into a memory of Queen Isolda at her daughter's wedding, face swollen with fury. "Only when provoked," he admitted. Then he thought on it a little more: all those countries falling under the sway of the Britannian Empire. "It's a complicated question."

The boy's eyes narrowed, taking on a narrow and foxy appearance that did not resemble Dashmond Gloucester at all. "Mine sent me through a reflection," he said. "Into a tree of bronze. Easy enough to do if you leave your body behind. I trusted her to keep my body safe while I did her bidding, and she did *this*. What kind of queen would act thus?"

One who plans ahead, Rinaldo thought. He had to hope that fairies had no ability to read minds.

What was her name, this wicked fairy who had murdered a cook and stolen more than one body? Quicksilver.

"When did you take the boy?" he asked. Flavia would be devastated to find her murdering fairy inside the child she wanted to protect so badly. Perrault Gloucester, at least, had survived the process, though he had looked quite traumatised when Rinaldo saw him recently.

"I released the man when we crossed over," said Dashmond — Quicksilver — with a ghost of a smile. "I could feel my own body calling out to me, so I let him go. Found myself trapped inside this inadequate, broken thing. Not for long. I was rescued by a much better option." She patted herself on the shoulder, looking satisfied. "Little Dash Gloucester, so brave and curious. He has the future of Empire ahead of him. Years of school, during which I can learn their ways. A good marriage in due course, tying me to one of the best families in London. He will be an Earl eventually, rich and powerful. I will be very comfortable in his skin."

"All you have to do is steal the body of a child."

Quicksilver smiled with Dashmond's mouth. "Easy as dancing."

A sound shivered through the forest around them, like a song or a scream. Quicksilver tilted her head and vanished into thin air. She still had magic, then, despite being in the boy's body. Or was she using the boy's own sparks?

Rinaldo looked down again at the smashed remains of Quicksilver's original body. Every instinct was screaming that he should rebuild the thing: offer the fairy a viable alternative to Dashmond. There was no metal available, but if he imagined hard enough that the leaves and twigs were copper wire and steel rods, he could probably form a working automaton from the pieces. Making a man's shape came easily to him; he had done it before.

But the materials were not right. The grass remained limply in his fingers. He needed metal!

After a thought, Rinaldo dug his hands into the rich, reddish earth beneath the grass, and let it fall through his fingers. There was iron in soil, was there not? Especially soil of such a healthy colour.

He scattered dirt over the shape of smashed dust where an arm used to be, creating a long nodule and several small coils. They hovered in the air, close to forming a connection, then fell lifelessly to the grass.

It was of no use. Without Orlando, Rinaldo had never had much luck in breathing life into automata. To truly breathe life and movement into a body required both of their magic combined. He needed his brother.

He was useless without him.

~

Flavia located Orlando a few doors down from the laboratory, in a smoking room designed in the expectation no lady would enter: all polished wood and green leather with nary a cushion or an antimacassar in sight.

Even the portrait was of the last King of Britannia: George IV, father of Charlotte I and grandfather of Isolda I.

Orlando stood at the window, gazing out at the city street below. He smoked a foul-smelling cheroot as if it was the last thing he would taste before going to the scaffold.

"Where in heaven's name did you get such a thing?" Flavia was tempted to open a window to let the smell out of the room, but this was London. Chances were high that the street outside smelled worse.

Orlando gave her an aloof look. "This is a gentlemen's club. Port and brandy in every room, and something to smoke in every other drawer."

"Let's leave the port and brandy where they are until this work is done," said Flavia. "We don't have a lot of time..."

"I'm aware," he snapped, and immediately apologised for being rude. "I'm worried about Rinaldo."

"I'm worried about all of them. Faerie is not a safe place for mortals." They were running out of time. Not that there had been spare time to begin with. They could not expect Tanaquil Gloriana to hold still and behave herself when there were humans in her territory. If Flavia's dream was true, then Queenie had already been captured.

Flavia had lost an arm when she last met her mother.

"He'd be furious at me for endangering the princess," murmured Orlando.

Flavia nodded slowly. "It seems as if the three of you were quite friendly, before all this."

"Friendly," he repeated blankly, with none of the roguish air she was used to from Orlando Device. "You know the story, I suppose?"

Flavia was unsure what he might mean. "About the princess?"

"About how the Empress of Britannia took two wayward, foreign orphan boys into her personal household and sponsored them as her Royal Engineers." Orlando sounded bitter.

"Oh," said Flavia, surprised. "Not really. My former employers at Dorchester Grove adored society gossip, so I heard quite a bit about Princess Ygraine and her sisters over the years. I suppose there must have been mention of you and Rinaldo as well, but I didn't pay a great deal of attention."

Orlando gave her an odd sort of smile. "It's rare for us to meet people who don't already have ideas about us. Preconceptions."

"A pretty way of saying cruelty and ignorance," Flavia said sharply.

Orlando puffed on the cheroot again, filling the air around them with detestable smoke. He couldn't possibly be enjoying it.

"It wasn't true, about Queen Isolda," Orlando said after a moment. "It was her cousin's husband who took us in. Albert, Duke of Bath. After he died, her Majesty could have thrown us out into the street, but Ygraine helped us to prove our usefulness. The Queen agreed to sponsor us, allowed us to create marvellous devices in her name. Royal Engineers. Higher than anyone ever thought we'd rise. And we ballsed it up, good and proper."

Flavia was becoming oddly used to his colourful turn of language. "I'm sure her Majesty knows how grateful you are..."

"We're not, though, are we?" he said bluntly. "We wrecked her daughter's wedding. Her Majesty locked us up in the Tower of London and we ran away rather than face her justice. Tonight, I damn near got Ygraine killed. How does that show gratitude to the patron who took a chance on us?" He took one last shaky draw of the cheroot. To Flavia's great relief, he then stubbed it out in a copper dish by his elbow. "How is she?"

"The princess is perfectly well for now," said Flavia. "You've nothing to worry about."

Orlando barked a short laugh. "Rinaldo does all the worrying, usually. I never realised how much work it is." He reached out blindly, caught up one of Flavia's gloved hands, and grazed his mouth briefly across the knuckles. "What would we do without you, Miss Wednesday?"

"You'll have to find out sooner or later," she said, putting a little stern into her voice as she tugged her hand back to herself. "You are too old for a governess to have any lasting effect on your behaviour."

Orlando laughed, more genuinely this time. It reached his dark eyes, at least. "Back to work," he said, and dropped her hand before loping back to the laboratory.

~

The first thing they saw was Princess Ygraine, sitting at the work bench near Cavendish the alchemist with a half-drunk cup of tea before her.

"What the buggering hell?" Orlando howled.

"I didn't think you'd mind if I drank from your cup," Ygraine said primly. "Mine was broken, and I had a funny taste in my throat that I needed to wash away."

Orlando turned on Cavendish in his fury. "You did this again?"

"Science," the alchemist said as if that was a reasonable excuse for anything.

"Really, Orlando," said the princess, back to her usual sharp self. "What a fuss to make over a cup of tea. I'm hardly going to ask your permission, am I? You're not a real person."

The expression on Orlando's face was awful. Flavia caught at his sleeve. "What is she talking about?"

Orlando was frozen for a moment. "I think that one's the Water of Truth, Cavendish," he said finally.

"Got it!" said the alchemist, sounding delighted. He made a note. "See, Miss Wednesday, I'm labelling the vial. No one can say I don't learn from my errors."

"Good for you," said Flavia, barely listening to him. "Well done, that alchemist. Orlando, what does she mean you're not a real person?"

"His brother made him out of iron filings and cake forks," said Ygraine. She started to laugh, and kept on laughing quite helplessly until Orlando Device spooned the Water of Undoing into her mouth himself.

~

When Rinaldo was working, the world fell away. Thread by thread, he drew the iron from the earth and shaped it into fibres that joined together each broken piece of the fairy Quicksilver's abandoned body.

Making things, *fixing things* made sense to him like nothing else in the world... even when this wasn't his world.

It might have been hours or days passing as Rinaldo worked. Here in Faerie, he felt little in the way of hunger or thirst. Perfect working conditions for an obsessive metallurmage. The need for supper or sleep or the water closet were such a bore, in the usual way of things.

Quicksilver's face gave him the greatest difficulty. Some of the fragments were smaller than a fingernail. Still, Rinaldo worked on it, piece by piece, lost in deep concentration as he discovered this new and fascinating thing he could do with his magic.

Flavia had made an arm from clover and grass. Rinaldo had made much more from much less. Making a person was...

Well, it wasn't the first time he had done this.

A soft pink cherry blossom fell on his face from above. Rinaldo wiped it away. His attention was gripped by the close work necessary to repair the broken fairy's face, one shard at a time. He was making minute connections now, with pinches of iron dust drawn from the earth at his feet.

Another blossom fell, and another. Rinaldo worked on. Finally, as the blossom rained prettily around him like a gentle snowstorm, he glanced up.

Three spindly trees had grown over him as he worked, bent heavy with the weight of flowers. The branches were thick with blossom that grew as quickly as the petals fell to the ground.

He had not noticed the prison growing around him. How long had he been here?

"You're very clever," said a voice like a spring breeze.

Rinaldo spun around, to see her standing behind him.

A girl. It was only a girl, perhaps ten years old, wearing a ballet-style crinoline dress: white and floaty in layers and layers, all edged with the same pink blossom that fell from the roof of his cage. Her mask was formed from twisted brown branches. Her hair, tangled to her waist, was as dark as a night sky.

The girl danced forward on footsteps as light as tissue paper. "I would be impressed," she observed. "If I did not have a very good reason for breaking this courtier in the first place."

Rinaldo was still holding Quicksilver's half-repaired head in his hands. He did not know what to do with it now. "I'm sorry, I —" *Couldn't help myself.*

The girl blinked behind her hard brown mask.

Gentle eyes, a darting smile. "Don't you know who I am?"

Rinaldo knew no fairies, apart from the murderous Quicksilver, and Flavia, who was nothing like this girl. There had been a play once, he recalled, at a Royal festival, something from Shakespeare about Midsummer. Full of names of famous fairies. Queen Isolda had banned it before opening night, and when she found there was a copy of the play in the palace library, she had confiscated that too.

Flavia was a fairy, he remembered belatedly, but she didn't belong here, in this place of spindly trees and plants and masks. She was too solid. This world was built on fragile dreams. There was nothing fragile about Flavia Wednesday.

Quicksilver's face fell apart in Rinaldo's hands, the pieces tumbling back on to the grass like cherry blossom petals. The filaments that Rinaldo had used to connect the pieces dissolved into dirt.

"She was not worthy," said the magnolia girl with an edge to her voice.

Rinaldo guessed then, who she was. "You're Gloriana," he said without thinking.

Queens should be taller, surely. His own queen, the Empress Isolda, was a rangy and wide-shouldered woman who chose gowns that made her look larger than she was, all skirts and collars and stiffened lace, using the modern fashions to emulate the past. Isolda would love nothing more than to be mistaken for the stately brocaded galleon that had been Good Queen Bess, last of the Tudors.

This fairy queen was half the size of Flavia; smaller even than Queenie. Her feet were bare, and her movements childlike. She arched up, her eyes blazing at him with anger and righteousness and, yes, power. "Tanaquil Gloriana," she raged, the branches of her mask turning black and grey even as fury burned in her eyes. "You will call me Majesty."

"Of course, your Majesty." Rinaldo bowed belatedly, with a great deal of flourish. Dealing with angry queens was something with which he had experience.

Tanaquil Gloriana giggled like a fairy from one of those silly children's books, the kind Rinaldo left for the girls to read back at the orphanage. *Merry Fairy Tiptoe Meets a Hedgehog*, and all that rot. *Darling Daisy Elf Lost Her Acorn. Tiny Tanaquil Smashes Heads and Eats an Engineer for Breakfast.*

"There's no iron here," said the little girl. "But you still found your magic, buried in the dirt. Sly of you. Too clever, I'm afraid."

Rinaldo brushed dirt across his bare, calloused hands. "Too clever for what?" he asked.

"Too clever to live," said the Queen of the Fairies.

Ygraine
Worrying about Orlando

"You know how Mr Albert had a closed coffin?" Orlando asked abruptly one day, in the middle of explaining how steam engines had changed the cotton industry.

I stilled. Was he finally willing to explain what was going on? Every time I walked in on the brothers it felt like I had interrupted some dire conversation about the end of the world. "I suppose."

"It's unusual, isn't it? In toff society. They like to stare at the corpse as long as possible, up to a week sometimes." Funny how his accent sometimes slipped. Orlando had taken to elocution like a duck to water, grasping how useful it was for a showman to be seen as cultured, educated. But you couldn't say a word like 'toff' while sounding like a marquess.

"You're horrid," I said, pulling a face. "What of it?"

"I know you saw," he said, his dark eyes holding mine. "A few weeks ago. When Rinaldo and I..."

A red stain spreading over his skin.

I took a deep breath. "Orlando, is something wrong with you? Are you ill?"

He gave me a long, searching look, then unbuttoned his cuff. He shoved up one white sleeve to show the markings: dark rust in a steady pattern along the vein of his light brown arm. It didn't look natural. It didn't look like anything I'd ever seen before.

"What is it?" I asked. I wanted to drag my fingertips along the strange pattern, but held myself back. When you've been trained all your life to avoid scandal, certain instincts squash themselves. It's like having a dozen governesses in your head at all times.

"Don't know," Orlando muttered. "I've been trying to figure it out. I think it has something to do our sparks, but I've never heard of it, not in any of the books. It got him. Mr Albert. It came on him like this, slow at first. By the time he dropped, it had reached his neck and face."

"It's caused by the metal you work with?" I repeated. "Which metal? Can you avoid it?"

Orlando shook his head slowly. "It's the magic, not the metal. Some kind of contamination. I wish I knew. Don't tell Rinaldo it's getting worse. I'll sort it out."

"He should know. He could help you." Surely someone could help him. "We can call a doctor, Mama has several..."

"No one can help me but me," Orlando said sharply. "Don't let him blame himself if it gets bad."

I blinked at him, thinking of Uncle Albert and his stomach. "How bad is it going to get?"

Orlando turned away. I threw myself at him, wrapping my arms around his shoulders in a breathless hug. All the governesses in my head could jolly well take their half day off. "If it's the magic doing this to you, you must stop using magic," I breathed into his neck.

He smelled like warm metal and engine oil.

"I'd die without magic," said Orlando, shrugging out from under my exceedingly improper embrace. "It's the only thing worth doing in the world. Pass me the number 8 screwdriver, will you, there's a good girl?"

I sharpened my expression at him. "I'm a princess. You keep forgetting that."

"Fine," said Orlando Device, as if he hadn't revealed something terrible to me. "Be a good *princess* and pass me the bloody screwdriver."

The first elf made her house out of twigs and laughed as the wind blew through the cracks.

The second elf made her house out of mud, building up walls with handfuls of wet river dirt.

The third elf made her house out of flowers which shone every colour in the sunshine.

"Careful, little elves," said the big bad goblin. "I'm coming to make you cry."[1]

— Primula Millicent Wednesday, *Sweet Peas in the Morning*, undated

---

1. This unpublished manuscript was found after the author's death along with a note from her editor suggesting it was *'a bit dark for the tots — couldn't we have something a bit more like Acorn's Dear Little Tea Party?'*

Chapter 7

In Which Our Travellers Take the Waters (and the Plunge)

Orlando and Cavendish barely stopped working long enough to bolt down a late supper of cheese, sandwiches and small cakes.

Ygraine, tired and irritable after being dosed and cured twice over, dropped off to sleep on the same little reading couch where Flavia had previously dozed. She did not appear to remember having said anything strange about Orlando, and merely frowned when Flavia hinted at it.

Orlando likewise made no effort to explain nor acknowledge Ygraine's strange declaration. He was lost in his own thoughts, his mouth a grim line.

Flavia would not let herself sleep. She had no wish to drop back into Faerie though dreams, not now that she was so close to crossing over in person. She was a tight-wound ball of anxiety at the very possibility that she might, with her own earthly body, set foot upon the glorious land that had created her.

(And come face to face with the queen who wanted her dead, of course, never forget that.)

Instead of sleeping, Flavia watched Orlando Device.

What the princess said could not possibly be true. How could Orlando, of all people, be one of Rinaldo's automata? His skin was warm; she remembered feeling the touch of his mouth to the back of her hand, even through the thin silk glove. She remembered the soft grip of his arm in hers as they strode across the city together.

If he was made of metal, I would feel it. I wouldn't be able to be near him.

Unless of course it was one of those metals which did not have an effect on the fey: copper, perhaps. Silver or gold. Anything that was not contaminated with cold iron.

He ate food, though. He drank liquid. Philtres had every effect on him. He breathed.

It could not be true.

"Don't look at me like that," he said irritably, some hours later.

Flavia was too tired and fizzing with nervous energy to be considerate of his feelings now. "Look at you like what?" she snipped.

"Like I am an exhibit in a museum."

"You look real enough to me."

Orlando put on a leering, ungentlemanly expression. "Shall I show you how real?"

"I would very much rather you did not," she said in her sternest of governess voices, and felt the heat of a blush cross her cheeks. How indecorous.

Orlando regarded her with sudden interest. "Do you know that you get a greenish shade across your cheeks when you blush?"

Flavia huffed. "Pointing out a lady's shortcomings is unworthy of you."

"Did I say shortcomings? I like your colour. It reminds me of a favourite shrubbery." There was no way that Orlando was not flesh and blood. He was too irritating to be anything but a real man.

Still, Flavia's thought had to be spoken out loud. "If there is iron inside you..."

Orlando pressed a hand to his chest. "Are you asking what lies beneath my clothing? What a scandal, Miss Wednesday."

"Don't be coarse!" she said crossly. "I know you're just trying to put me off the scent."

"Am I?"

She took a deep breath. "Perhaps you should not go to Faerie."

Now she had his attention. "You expect me to let you wander off into the greenwood without my company?"

"It's hardly a question of *let*. I'm far better

equipped to deal with that place than you are. And if..." She could not finish her absurd thought.

"Fairies don't like cold iron, so I hear," Orlando said, realising what she was getting at.

"Your magic won't work there," she tried.

"I shouldn't worry about that. My magic has been acting up for a while now."

"How reassuring."

How could his magic work at all, if... no. Ygraine must have been speaking in metaphor, that was all.

Orlando's voice was chilly now. "To be frank, *Miss Wednesday*, our motives for crossing over are not aligned. You wish to reclaim those children you neglected. I want my brother back, and the princess wants her husband. I don't believe for a moment you would choose to save either man if it were between them or the little ones."

Flavia lowered her gaze to the floor, feeling resentment burn all the way up from her toes. "I see," was all she said. It was true enough. The thought that Orlando would save his brother or the Duke of Cornwall over Queenie and Dash was rather infuriating.

She was not going to let him pick a fight with her, if that was his intention. They needed each other. She could not do this alone.

Orlando was still speaking. "I have not forgotten who your mother is, madam. She's your weakness, and she's not mine."

She had been prepared to keep the bridge of

friendship open between them, but calling her *madam* was too close to the bone.

"That settles it, then," Flavia said crisply. "We walk our own paths."

"Indeed," replied Orlando Device, and returned to his work with Cavendish, leaving her with more questions, and no answers.

~

F aerie had well and truly got its hooks into Rinaldo. He found himself bouncing along inside a cage made of those same pink-blossomed branches, carried by several spindly-armed creatures with dark laughing eyes and wicked, pinching fingers. Were these pixies, perhaps? He had made no study of the different types of fairy, but they were only knee-high. They didn't seem to speak his language, only chittered to each other. He was going to call them pixies for now. If he was wrong, no one would know.

The cage was another flashback to Rinaldo's mortal life, facing the wrath of Empress Isolda on the day after her daughter's wedding. This was, he had to admit, a less awful prison than the grim little cell in the Tower of London, or indeed the cellar underneath Number 12 Actaeon Place where he had been kept by Lady Mortmain alongside the storage barrels and a whole side of beef.

Here, at least the sunshine was on his face, and the

air was not stale. The sunshine did not feel especially warm, and the air did not taste of anything Rinaldo recognised, but it could be worse.

He was bumped and jostled along in the cherry blossom cage, carted through trees and thickets and then across a stream deep enough that his boots and the cuffs of his trousers were thoroughly soaked.

When the creatures on one side of the cage tired of his weight, they jabbed him through the bars until he settled himself on the other side, which made the other pixies groan and, after a while, pinch to move him over again.

He was ready to make pixie soup by the end of it, or to build a glorious metal machine that turned the blighters into fat sausages.

It was a long while since Rinaldo had eaten. Now that he had no work to fixate upon, the Faerie trick of concealing human needs seemed to have worn off. His stomach felt scraped inside out.

"Here, then!" cried the girlish, imperious voice of Tanaquil Gloriana. "Let's see our prisoner dance."

The cage fell away. Rinaldo was expelled with great force, rolling and tumbling across the grass. His palms hummed as they grazed the ground — the dirt of this strange land had recognised something in him and liked it.

Slowly, pretending to be more disoriented than he was, Rinaldo looked around the clearing through lidded eyes. Fairies. Pixies. All manner of other winged and masked creatures, staring at him like he was a prize on display. It was like being perused by a hungry squadron of owls while disguised as a tasty worm.

Rinaldo rose slowly to his feet, his eyes falling upon on a bizarre concoction of trees and turf and flowers and... it was a house. A house that looked a lot like Number 12 Actaeon Place, although it was smaller in all proportions. Barely large enough for him to stand at full height in each room. It reminded him of the bronze fountain that he had built in his sleep and destroyed only moments before arriving here. "Who built this?" he asked, to buy time.

A girl's face appeared at a window made from coiled branches. "Mr Device, is that you?" she called.

Queenie. "Miss Gloucester," he called to her. "Don't worry. I'll get you out."

The fairies laughed, all of them.

"You're the one who should worry," said the Queen of the Fairies in a vicious twinkle of a voice. "We need that girl. Her blood will give us safe passage into the world of men."

"Are you saying you have no use for me?" Rinaldo asked, knowing a veiled threat when he heard one.

"Oh," said Tanaquil Gloriana, batting her lashes at him like he had promised to buy her an ice from the fair. "You have a use, Mr Device." She passed him a bronze blade, shaped like a leaf. Wicked sharp, it gleamed in the palm of his hand.

Surely a trick. Rinaldo opened his hand to drop the

knife, but it clung to him like it was magnetised. He curled his fingers back around the hilt, not strong enough to relinquish it a second time. Metal. He felt stronger now, more capable. "What do you need me to do?" he asked in a voice that felt hardly his own.

The Queen of the Fairies let out a trill of triumph. "We need you to spill that blood of hers. Make as much mess as you like."

~

"Done!" announced Cavendish, surveying the series of vials and beakers with some satisfaction. The waters of the enchanted fountains of the Forest of Arden, all lined up in a row.

Flavia stepped forward, with Ygraine close behind her. "What do we do now?"

"What's the catch?" added Ygraine.

Orlando scattered clockwork beetles across the table and filled them, one at a time, from the different vials and beakers. "Miss Wednesday, if you please."

Flavia stepped closer to him and folded her arms over her bosom, daring him to impress her.

Orlando dropped clockwork beetles into her cupped hands, two for Flavia, two for Ygraine. He had used some of the equipment and ingredients here to alter the natural colour of the beetles in different metallic colours, so they could actually tell the difference between them — a terribly good idea which

145

begged the question why he hadn't thought of it the first time around. "The blue one is the Water of Worlds. You'll drink half to travel and save the other half for your ticket home. The copper one is the Water of Undoing — keep that one close to your heart, it may be the most useful thing you've ever held."

The beetles had claws that could clip on to any cord or ribbon. Flavia turned away in order to secret the copper beetle on to the laces of her corset, beneath her dress. Thankfully, it did not wriggle any of its little metallic legs.

Cavendish said nothing, but regarded Flavia as if he had just heard she had the consumption.

"Orlando," said the Princess Ygraine sharply. "What aren't you telling us about these philtres?"

Orlando looked ashamed of himself, even as he gave Ygraine the same beetles he had given to Flavia: blue for Water of Worlds, copper for Water of Undoing. Ygraine tucked them into the reticule she had pinned to her dress with a rather expensive brooch, and then wrapped herself back into her swathes of silken cloak, awaiting Orlando's reply.

"Our success rate was not what we hoped," Orlando admitted. "There's a possibility of trace contamination between the philtres."

"If only my hands were a mite steadier," lamented Cavendish with a meaningful groan.

"Yes," Orlando snarled back at him, filling his own pockets with clockwork beetles, dozens of them, in a far more hues than he had provided to the two young ladies. "Believe me, I regret keeping you from your gin."

"Cross contamination," said Flavia. "Does that mean..."

"Other philtres might well be present in each dose of the Water of Worlds," Orlando said with a deep sigh. "As you might remember, a tiny amount of a philtre of Arden can replicate itself in a larger quantity of liquid."

Flavia sighed as well, looking at the now ominous blue beetle in her hands. "Death, oblivion, transformation," she recited. Surely, they were the three worst possibilities.

"It is a risk," agreed Orlando. "And one I am content to make alone if you have both changed your minds about crossing over."

Flavia looked at Ygraine. She knew why she was going: she would not be able to breathe properly again until the Gloucester children were home and safe. Perhaps Ygraine felt the same about the Duke of Cornwall, or perhaps she was merely a spoiled princess seeking an adventure. It was hard to tell.

It did not matter to Flavia whether Orlando was made of flesh or teaspoons. He would stop at nothing to save his brother. Flavia liked Rinaldo very much, but for her the children were always going to come first.

Queenie. Dash. I'm coming for you.

Orlando held his own blue clockwork beetle out in

ceremonious fashion, as if proposing a toast. "Miss Wednesday, we are relying on you. Everything I have ever read about the Water of Worlds states that you can only travel to a place you can see in your mind. Her high — this lady and I have not been to Faerie. We're going to have to ride on your coat-tails."

Flavia opened her mouth to argue that she had never travelled bodily to Faerie herself, but decided against it. What were all those dreams for, over the years, if not preparing her for this? She knew the land well. She could find it with her eyes closed and the world on fire.

Orlando held out his other hand, palm-up. Flavia laid her hand over his, feeling the warmth of his skin. He felt like flesh and blood beneath the softness of her palm. What had Ygraine meant when she spoke under the influence of the Water of Truth?

His brother made him out of iron filings and cake forks.

Orlando's dark eyes held hers for a moment, and then he looked to Ygraine. She laid her own cool hand over Flavia's. "To Faerie then," the princess said, as if she had never been afraid of anything in her life.

Faerie, thought Flavia, conjuring it up in her mind. She pictured the trees, so many you could never count them all, the grasses and the rivers. She thought of the greenwoods full of song and laughter, of the flowers and the many masks and the deep longing she had always felt to stand among her own people. To dance their songs and breathe their air.

Home, I'm coming home.

Flavia held the Isle of Faerie in her thoughts and gave a brisk nod to show Orlando that she was ready. He flicked open the tiny metal flask shaped like a beetle, and the ladies followed suit. All three of them drank in the same instant. Half a swallow, no more. Save some for the return journey...

Faerie. Home. Now.

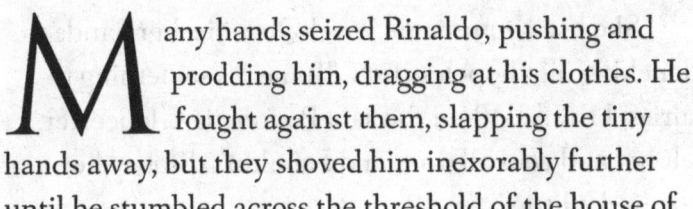

Many hands seized Rinaldo, pushing and prodding him, dragging at his clothes. He fought against them, slapping the tiny hands away, but they shoved him inexorably further until he stumbled across the threshold of the house of flowers.

Once he was in, they slammed the woven door closed again, chanting and singing. "Kill her, stab her, eat her alive." Faces loomed at him through the gaps in the woven branches and spiralling vines: hungry eyes, sharp-toothed mouths.

Queenie Gloucester stood in her long white nightie at the far end of the room, framed by a wall of braided lavender, comfrey and bright tropical flowers. As Rinaldo looked at her, she raised her chin a little. Brave girl.

"Your choice is simple, Mr Device," said the voice of the Queen, echoing through the house of flowers. "Spill the girl's blood, and we can all return to the mortal country. You may return to your human life of beer and tea leaves and kidney pudding and frigging and gambling and counting metal coins and everything else that mortal men enjoy. Or... you can let her live and die of old age right here in this glorious land of ours. We're fairies, Rinaldo. We have nothing but time."

"I feel a little insulted," Rinaldo said in a low voice, not quite managing a laugh. "That's what she thinks humans do all day?"

"She used your name," said Queenie, her hands clenching into hopeless fists. "It means something to fairies, I think. When she said Petronella Gloucester, I felt hot and cold all over, and I couldn't disobey her, not even a little."

"That's all right," said Rinaldo, thinking of a small boy in an orphanage. "Rinaldo's not properly my name."

It was an odd system. Why should fairy magic hold power over you when they used a name that didn't even fit any more? 'Queenie' should work better than 'Petronella,' being the name she chose for herself.

Not that I chose my name, he thought, a little unfairly. Like everything else in his life, that had been Orlando's idea.

Rinaldo squeezed the hilt of the bronze blade

between his fingers. He glanced up and around. No urge to murder a child had taken him over. "How many rooms in this place?"

"Sixteen," said Queenie, her voice low and terrified. She could not take her eyes off the knife in his hand. He could not blame her for that. "I counted. Sixteen rooms including a cellar and a double attic, plus some rather narrow corridors."

Rinaldo nodded to himself. He met Queenie's eyes and tried to look as harmless as possible. "Trust me," he promised in a quiet murmur. "I won't hurt you." Much louder, he said, "Start running, Miss Gloucester!"

The fairy crowd whooped and hollered as Queenie fled through the nearest doorway. She shoved aside a curtain of weeping willow fronds to make her escape. Rinaldo stalked after her, the knife held high, feeling every bit like the villain they expected him to be.

He had to draw this out as long as possible. Once Tanaquil and her creatures realised he was not playing their game, they were sure to change the rules.

Have they ever met a human before? Do they think it is so easy, to turn us into monsters?

Flavia stumbled, overwhelmed by scent and colour. Warmth. There was no warmth like this in England. Not anywhere in mortal Britannia.

The ground tipped up to meet her, and when she splayed out her hands, she felt the earth warm under her gloved fingers. She peeled off the gloves in a moment, shoving them into a pocket sewn into the side of her day dress.

Now she could bury her bare fingers into the lush green grass of Faerie. Flavia's flower arm drank in the magic of this land. *Home*. The grass had a bright, wet scent, like no grass she had ever smelled before. She wanted to roll around in it, naked. There was no place for corsetry here. Her day dress felt tight, unnecessary.

If I open my eyes, it won't be true.

Every breath brought in tastes and scents that Flavia had longed for, stronger and sweeter than ever. Apples, mint, fresh liquorice root. Acorns and spring blossom, wintergreen and summer roses. Other scents she could not recognise: fruits and flowers she'd never even heard of.

"It's you," said a voice.

Flavia looked up and caught the troubled eyes of the princess. Ygraine, pale-faced and swathed in midnight blue silk, stared at her like she had seen an illustration in a storybook come to life.

"You're *green*," Ygraine said, eyes wide. "Green all

over. And oh, your arm." She didn't sound disgusted, at least. Curious, if anything.

As Flavia rose to her feet, Ygraine's face twisted in pain and she turned away, covering her face with her hood. "Oh!"

"What's wrong?"

The silk cloak billowed as if there was a wild breeze, though Flavia had not felt the air stir.

"Ygraine," she said, lunging forward to grasp the cloak. It came away in her hand, loose and empty.

A black crow with sharp yellow eyes flapped out of the silk cloak and took off into the air.

"Transformation," said Orlando, at Flavia's elbow. "Damn."

The waters had been contaminated... and they'd lost the princess already.

It was worse than that. Flavia realised it as she turned to look at Orlando Device.

"Not the best start," he admitted.

Rage darkened the edge of her vision. How could she ever have thought he was handsome? His face turned her stomach, made her wanted to slap it, bite it. He had always been infuriating, but she had never felt like this before.

"Don't worry," said Orlando, ignoring her distress like the monster he was. "The Water of Undoing will fix her right up."

"Don't come near me!" Flavia snarled. Fury sparked off every hair on her body. She wanted to light

him on fire. She couldn't trust anything he gave her to
drink.

"What's wrong?" He obeyed, at least, his eyes fixed
on her. His smile was softer than it should be, his eyes
brighter.

The effect was grotesque enough that Flavia forced
her eyes shut. "Orlando," she whispered. "We have to
look for Rinaldo and the children on our own. Run as
far and as fast from me as you can."

"Is this the crow thing? Because I'm pretty sure
that's only forty percent my fault."

He was too near. She felt his hand brush her arm,
and revulsion shook her body. Too late to fight the
philtre now.

"Flavia, look at me," he said in a low voice. "I have
to know..."

Flavia breathed out a lungful of sweet Faerie air
and opened her eyes to gaze directly into the eyes of
Orlando Device.

I hate him so much I can't breathe with it.

Ygraine

a pointless distraction

One week before my seventeenth birthday, I found out about Archibalt Lyonesse. He was Viscount Lyon, the last surviving heir to the duchies of Cornwall and Land's End, and now my betrothed.

It could have been worse.

Once you set aside the ill-luck association of his family with mine (he had been cousin to Tristan, the man who doomed my sister), Archie was as suitable as any other landed gentleman of Britannia. Better Cornwall than being packed off to Bavaria like Unity, or to the Orkneys like Evanna.

I'd known Archie for years. There had been talk of marrying him to Unity, before she got a better offer. He was *fine*. His face was symmetrical, with a nose that just about added character without making him look like a newspaper cartoon. He made amiable conversation at table and dressed well (though that speaks of his

competent valet rather than any personal achieve-
ment). He was only half a dozen years older than me.
Best of all, he did not have the air of a man who was
likely to strangle his wife, or trail actresses through
their summer home the moment her back was turned.

As a future husband, he was acceptable.

There was no rush for a wedding. The current
Duke, Archie's father, saw no need for me to be
married straight out of the school room. I had years yet
to roam around Buckingham Palace doing nothing and
being useful to no one.

I had no reason to feel distress. This was what
happened to all young ladies, especially princesses.
Who needed love? Love nearly made Mama lose
herself when Papa died. Cousin Victoria still showed
no sign of recovering from the loss of Uncle Albert. A
nice, sensible marriage was exactly the ticket.

If I did decide I wanted a love match, then I had
years to make myself fall in love with the future Duke
of Cornwall and Land's End... and if that didn't work,
well.

There was always a love philtre.

All was well, and there was absolutely no reason
why I should be awake after midnight, staring at my
ceiling and panicking about my future.

My head was full of Iseult, Oonagh, Evanna. My
three dead sisters. I felt like I was going to explode.

What I most wanted to do was to sit on a bench in the

workshop beneath Buckingham Palace and listen to Orlando Device being sarcastic at me. He was the only person in the world who regularly forgot I was a princess...

But it was Rinaldo who met me at the door. He looked rough and unshaven; his eyes bleary with lack of sleep. He smelled like metal, rust and sweat. I'd never seen him so unkempt! "You can't come in," he muttered. "We're in the middle of an experiment."

"I want to see Orlando," I insisted.

A haunted look crossed Rinaldo's face. "You can't. He's busy."

I thought of the discoloured metallic smear spreading across Orlando's chest, the secret he had confided in me. Worry pricked at me. "Let me in."

"No," Rinaldo snapped, already pushing the door closed. "Stay out of this. You don't belong here."

I stared at the door which had never been closed to me before. I wanted to pound on it with my fists. It wasn't like the Device brothers to use the fact that they were bigger against me.

(Not that I had any compunction in using the power I had against them.)

"The Royal Engineers are both invited to my birthday ball next week," I said loudly. "If Orlando's not there, I will know there is something wrong and *I will tell my mother*."

"You've used that threat too often, highness," said Rinaldo, his voice muffled by the door. "Orlando will be at your damned ball. Now leave me — leave us alone."

~

I dreamed of a grail full of flowers. I dreamed of Orlando dancing in a garden with bright silver eyes. *He's alive, at least*, I thought as I awoke. *If he's dancing, that means he's alive.*

~

At breakfast the next morning, Mama spoke to me for the first time in weeks, glancing over a plate of kedgeree as if she had only just noticed I was still here. "You will not return to that workshop," she said.

I startled. "Has someone complained about me?" Rinaldo, that snake.

"It's not appropriate for an engaged woman, Ygraine. You must think of your future."

My future as Viscountess Lyon was so far away, I could barely imagine what it would look like. The future after *that*, as the Duchess of Cornwall and Land's End, might as well have been something out of a fairy tale.

"Did Orlando and Rinaldo ask you to keep me away?" I demanded, hot all over. After all my kindnesses to them... to treat me as some kind of nuisance. To go to my *mother*.

"Their work is essential for the Empire," said Queen Isolda, as if that was an end to the matter. "Really, child. Can't you open a hospital or work with your father's Exhibition, if you must find something useful to do? It's not like you are anything more than a pointless distraction to my Royal Engineers."

Later that morning, this pointless distraction knocked on the workshop door for half an hour, until my hands hurt. Neither Rinaldo nor Orlando acknowledged my existence.

What happened to them was that there are two springs

 Off in the Ardennes, not far apart,
 And drinking the waters of one of them always brings

 Love and longing to the drinker's heart,
 But as you have guessed already, knowing how things

 Often work, the other waters will start
 A hatred in one who has tasted them. And these

 Two imbibed the contraries

— Ludovico Ariosto, *Orlando Furioso*,
1532 (transl. David R. Slavitt 2009)

Chapter 8

In Which Our Travellers Encounter a Strange and Glorious Land

Revulsion burned in Flavia's stomach, and bile pricked at her tongue. Orlando Device stood before her on the wild grasslands of Faerie as if he had done nothing to deserve her ire. Why was he even here?

How dare he be alive?

"If you're worried about Ygraine," he started to say, but even that was too much.

Flavia sprang at him, her hands grabbing at his throat. She had no idea how to throttle someone, and the feel of his warm body beneath the starchy shirt collar made her own skin crawl.

Her flower hand was stronger than it looked; all those dandelions woven together, finally good for something.

Orlando deflected her easily, holding her wrists in

his strong engineer's hands as she hung off him like a paper doll. "Flavia, stop."

"Don't touch me!"

"You grabbed me first!" His eyes were luminous as he gazed at her, and of all things a stupid smile teased across his face. As if her rage was attractive. Adorable. Desired.

Ugh.

Flavia resorted to her governess voice. "Let me go," she ordered him.

Orlando released her hands instantly. Flavia twisted away. Her whole body shook with fear and disgust. *Casting up your accounts, isn't that what they call it, when you're so sickened that you...* She pressed both hands to her mouth. "Orlando, I hate you," she whispered between her fingers.

"You wouldn't be the first," he said lightly. "If this is your way of letting me down easily, my dear, I must congratulate you on your original take. Usually I just get a tankard of beer over my head..."

Letting him down? What on earth was he thinking? "The philtres, you imbecile," Flavia said between gritted teeth. "The contaminated water. Isn't there a Water of Hate?"

"Ah," Orlando said. A long, slow silence unfurled around them. "Inconvenient."

"We won't be able to travel together."

"No, I see that. But it's rather worse, I'm afraid."

"Orlando," she said, the anger rising again. Why couldn't he listen to her instead of dragging this out? "How could it be worse?"

He let out a heavy sigh. "I'm in love with you."

Flavia forced herself to make a sound, but it didn't come out like a laugh. More like half a scream. "Of course, you are." None of the philtres were pure. It was a miracle that any of them had made it to the Isle of Faerie alive.

"I know the signs, after all," Orlando went on. "Philtre-wise, this one is something of an old friend."

"I don't want to hear it." The thought of Orlando feeling that way about her was — well, if Flavia wasn't shaking with pure loathing, it might be almost funny. But she could hardly remember how it had felt to be his friend.

"Flavia," he said, sounding tortured.

"Miss Wednesday," Flavia snarled back.

"This would all be resolved quite easily if you were to drink the Water of Undoing. It's the..."

"I know which one it is." She reached into her dress, pulled the clockwork beetles out and threw them at him, one after the other. "Am I supposed to trust you now? Who is to say the Water of Undoing is not laced with Death, or Oblivion?"

"You're right, of course," Orlando agreed, gathering up the beetles in his large, ungainly hands. He hesitated over the last of these: the shiny blue beetle. "You should hang on to this one. The Water of Worlds. It's your only way home... and you know at least which philtre it's contaminated with. It's not like you can hate me *more*."

Flavia growled at him. "I want nothing that is yours."

Orlando large eyes looked wounded, as if she had stuck an arrow between his ribs. "I only want to help you." Because a philtre had made him think he was in love with her. What a colossal disaster this was.

"Fine," Flavia said, lifting her chin. She could use this to her advantage, at least. "If you love me so very much, Mr Device. Never mind your brother, or the wretched cat. If you get the slightest chance, save those children. Whatever it takes. Whatever it costs you. Get them back safely to Britannia. They are your priority now. Keep them away from my mother."

Orlando straightened, as if he was a knight of old, honoured to have received a quest from his lady. "As you will, Miss Wednesday."

Machine, he's a machine, he's a monster, made of scraps, you can't trust him...

Flavia nodded stiffly at Orlando and then turned and walked away. She didn't need him. She could rescue the children herself. She didn't need his magic. This was her land. Faerie.

She had spent her whole life wanting to be here, and now she was, and it was awful, and she was alone.

But she had a mission, and there was no point getting soppy about it.

One foot in front of the other, Wednesday. Buck up. Worse things happen at sea.

∼

R inaldo shouldered his way through the fragile house of flowers, sending petals and leaves flying as he thundered through the delicate rooms. The bronze knife was hot in his hand; bronze. Never mind the blade's edge, it felt good to have metal back again. It was a tool he hadn't thought to find here.

He'd lost Queenie somewhere in this maze of braided twigs, but he'd lost the peering eyes and grinning faces, too.

A low whistle caught his attention; he looked down. Queenie was a level below him, standing on a replica of the great staircase, sandwiched between what looked like thick slices of haystack.

She beckoned, then disappeared from sight.

Rinaldo half-climbed, half slid down to meet her.

They were in the heart of the house now; his hands remembered building it up out of bronze a lifetime ago. The lighting was dim, and the two of them took a moment to catch their breath.

"I assume you're not going to stab me," Queenie whispered.

"That depends," Rinaldo said, trying for a joke. "I assumed this was you luring me into a trap?" His eyes adjusted slowly to the lack of light. "Is this a *library*?"

It was certainly trying to be a library. The walls were formed from fruit trees, with long square-ish fruits lined up as if they were books. It was as if someone had seen a library once, then attempted to grow a replica in their garden.

Exactly like that.

"Three rooms or passageways on either side of us," whispered Queenie. "If there's anywhere in here those creatures can't see or hear us, this is it. Though if you don't produce any Gloucester blood, I'm sure she will send her people in after us. I hope you have a plan, Mr Device."

Rinaldo hoped so too. He should give her the knife, so that she knew not to be afraid of him, but it was the only metal in this benighted land, and he needed it. (He could feel his magic again, uncurling and ready to go to work.)

"Smart girl," he said finally.

"I try," said Queenie, with a world of cynicism in her young voice. "What are we going to do?"

Rinaldo stared at the bronze knife, thinking about it. A single drop of liquid fell on to the blade. He looked up, and saw more water welling in the woven ceiling; another droplet about to fall. "Does it rain in Faerie?" he said aloud.

"It must," said Queenie. "Surely. All these plants would not grow without it."

"It wasn't raining before. I've seen no rain since we arrived." Best not to think about how long that might have been.

Another drop fell, past his face to the floor.

"Where do the philtres come from?" Rinaldo asked, thinking aloud.

"A laboratory," Queenie said dourly.

"Not *your* philtres," he said with a quick smile for the budding scientist. "The ones in the fountains. The Forest of Arden — and Faerie — they used to be connected, before the exile. Could fairy magic have created those fountains, and the philtres inside? Magically imbued water couldn't just happen, surely."

"That's a very scientific suggestion," Queenie said, with grudging approval. "Apart from the magic, which is nonsense. What's your point?"

Rinaldo stared up at the droplets forming on the ceiling of woven flowers and fruit. "I was thinking — if that is anything other than pure rainwater, we might be in a lot of trouble."

The ceiling broke open, fronds of blossom and woven willow splitting apart, as water cascaded down over their heads.

∽

Hunting one crow in an endless island made up largely of forest was not the easiest task that Flavia had ever set for herself.

It became easier once she ditched the corset.

The air was so warm, and it felt wrong to wear constraining underthings here, in a land she associated with freedom and dancing.

She made absolutely certain that she was alone in a thicket before removing her dress and unlacing the sturdy corset. After a moment's thought, she took off her stockings and boots as well, bundling it all up together in Ygraine's abandoned silk cloak.

Flavia was not used to letting her skin be green without looking over her shoulder to worry about who might see. She wriggled her leaf-coloured toes into the lush grass with delight. Perhaps in the mortal world she would have to worry eventually about her soles not being tough enough to walk barefoot very far, but this was her country.

Her petticoats and bloomers would be enough to count as respectably clothed in a land where most of the inhabitants ran around naked except for garlands of flowers and wisps of cobwebby silk... but Flavia didn't want to startle the princess or Rinaldo if their paths crossed again. So, the acorn-brown day dress went on again, a little looser than before. Walking felt like less of a hardship after that.

There was so much walking. The grove of trees

turned out to be more of a wood that went on for a terribly long time, its branches shielding her from the sky.

Trees trees, she heard on the wind. *Leaf and breeze, stem and seed.* Sometimes when she walked through long grass, she felt tiny fingers grasping at her ankles, but no fairy or other creature approached her.

At one point, Flavia heard a cry from above that might be a crow, and walked faster.

She's going to kill you, whispered the birch trees. *She won't forgive what you've done, little Flaxenseed.*

Flavia emerged from the shade of the trees into bright sunshine and regretted the acorn day dress after all; she was still wearing too many layers. When she tipped her head up to the bright blue sky, she saw a black bird, circling.

It might not be Ygraine. But were there other birds in this land? She'd seen butterflies and dragonflies and tiny midges that stung at her skin, but nothing with feathers.

Flavia ran forward, waving her arms. A caw cut through the empty air, and the bird spiralled lower.

The grass was like velvet underfoot. Solid in a way that Flavia's dreams had never been solid, and yet still so terribly unreal. She was walking through a Tennyson poem, or an oil painting of Titania and her nymphs.

Of course, the first crow Flavia saw was a princess in disguise. There was no time-wasting in ballads.

The black bird swooped down, and became a dark-haired girl, running. Ygraine was pink in the face and exuberant; impossibly, she still wore her pretty dark blue gown, tight around the bodice and streaming out a train of ruched satin from her knees to her ankles. She came at Flavia in a full run, pulling herself up just short of a collision. "Goodness!" she said, gasping with laughter. "Have you taken off your corset?"

"I'm more impressed that you still have yours on," said Flavia.

Ygraine was so pretty here; laughter suited her, away from London. "Oh, I get a terrible backache without mine. But do you mean the transformation? I'd love to use magic to get all my underpinnings on every morning, I don't mind telling you! How did you take yours off without a maid?"

Flavia was not used to lovely girls wondering what she had on under her clothes; her only romance since she came of age had been the long and desperately one-sided pash she shared with Quicksilver, who had no interest in garments other than masks. She blushed now, then pulled herself together as she remembered that blushing only made her more green. "Are you all right? That philtre..."

"Oh, I could club Orlando over the head for that!" exclaimed Ygraine, a laugh still on her lips. "I was a *bird*. I've never done anything so miraculous in my life."

Flavia's ribs tightened at the mention of Orlando;

even with him out of sight, the mere mention had her hating him all over again. She knew it wasn't true, wasn't real, and yet her body shook with the power of it.

It was a good thing she hadn't been armed when the philtre took hold. She might so easily have stabbed him.

"Wait," she said. Ygraine had already turned away from her and was marching with determination in the direction of a hill covered in thick, wild greenery. "Where do you think are you going?"

"I saw something from above," said the princess. "I want to see if I was right. You don't have to come with me."

Everything in Flavia wanted to grab Ygraine, pull her away. But the truth was, she had no better idea where to go. She had thought that it would be easy to remember the paths, that coming here would immediately immerse her in the wild dance and the court of glories. She would know how to find the House of Flowers where Queenie was imprisoned, simply because this was Faerie and she knew this place.

(Flavia had also thought her mother might have sensed her presence by now, and made herself known.)

At least if they went up that slope, she might be able to see the land from above. Ygraine's idea was not a bad one.

"What are you looking for?" she asked as she hurried after the princess.

"A grail," said the other girl, her face still caught in the merriment of her crow transformation. "It's a sort of a fancy cup, from the old legends."

"I know what a *grail* is." Reading the tales that mortals spun about Faerie was something Flavia, at least, had spent many hours on. Even though she had every reason to suspect it was entirely made up. There must be something in it all, those stories that kept coming around. Thomas the Rhymer, Tam Lin, Shakespeare's Cobweb and Mustardseed... maybe even her great-aunt's awful books had kernels of truth to them. "Why do you care?"

"Because," said Ygraine, her smile wild and untamed. "I've been dreaming about grails half my life. Why do you think I followed you to Faerie?"

~

Water dripped over Rinaldo's face, into his mouth. He was in a hole, dug fresh with dirt, and everything between him and the sky was — branches, twigs, roses, vines, layers and layers of what had been the House of Flowers. He groaned and found himself in mud up to the waist. "Queenie?"

Somewhere, there was a giggle.

He struggled up, but the mud sucked him down.

"Mr Device," came a very small voice.

"I thought we agreed you could call me Rinaldo."

"A house fell on us."

More giggles, and some sly chattering though he couldn't see where it was coming from. "Are you in one piece?"

"Just about," said the girl, and he felt some rustling nearby. "What was that water? Was it really a philtre?"

Rinaldo stared at the bronze knife he still held; pushed it a little, to see if it responded to his magic.

It divided into three prongs; from knife to fork.

At the same time, the branch nearest his other hand sprang apart into three even pieces.

Rinaldo, frowning, braided the bronze with slow, careful curls of his mind. The branch and the bronze reacted in tandem, twisting around each other. "I think perhaps it was the Water of Transformation," he suggested.

Twigs exploded to his left, and Queenie stuck her head through the remains of a wall. Her braids were a wild tangle of bramble and mud. "Is that good?"

Rinaldo nodded, thinking hard. "I believe so."

"You'd better hurry with whatever it is you have in mind to get us out of here," she said. "I heard some pixies singing, and I don't have to have read fairy tales extensively to know that means something very creepy is going to happen."

Rinaldo breathed. He had bronze. He had his magic. He had a wide selection of building materials.

They were both soaked to the skin with something he was certain was a philtre for transforming things.

I can work with this.

T he hill was also a maze.

When Flavia dreamed of Faerie, it had been forests, rivers, rolling hills and wide open spaces. Glorious, terrible, and everything she ever craved in a home.

She had never dreamed it would contain walls.

But this particular hill — the one that Princess Ygraine had a fancy to climb — was thick with high, wild hedges.

Flavia knew mazes. Her former employer, Lady Earnsley of Dorchester Grove, had been obsessed with tidy, intricate gardens. She hired an army of clippers and savagers to regularly carve her greenery into complex mathematical patterns.

On clipping days, Flavia always elected to visit the villages, so as not to be near the hedges as they fell screaming under the secateurs.

This maze had been grown rather than clipped. The high green walls were rounded and uneven, with no flat or straight lines. The mossy paths between the walls dipped and flowed like the bed of a river, or the branches of a plum tree.

They were still walls.

Fairies loved to laugh, and mock, and tease. Nowhere was that more obvious than in this particular construction, which taunted them at every turn. Flavia had tried counting paths, and always turning right, and every other rule she had learned about navigating mazes with *logic*.

It did not work.

For the first — hour? Day? Endless eternity? What was time? — Princess Ygraine led the way with a determination that was surprising, considering that her little buttoned boots must be straining under so much exercise.

Eventually, her energy flagged under the heat of the sun that showed no sign of moving across the sky.

"Still hanging on to the corset?" Flavia asked when they stopped to rest.

Ygraine sagged against a yew hedge thick with bumblebees. "Honestly," she said, fanning herself with her hand. "I don't know how you stand up without one."

There were buttercups growing on this hedge in entirely the wrong way: soaring upwards like an ivy vine, forming a golden web of branching lines. Flavia frowned.

"I don't think this is real," she observed.

"I think you're right," Ygraine agreed. "But since my alternative is to turn back into a crow and fly there directly..."

"Could you?" Flavia asked, startled.

"I believe so. You still hate Orlando, don't you?"

Flavia thought about it, and the rage welled up inside her again. She pressed it down hastily. "What's so special about this grail?" she asked.

"I wish I knew," Ygraine huffed. "I've been dreaming of it for far too long to give up on it now. But it's the only thing about this place that feels like it's about me." She peered at Flavia. "You didn't have to come."

"I was hoping to find out more about where we are," Flavia admitted. "But I can't see anything with all these hedges around us."

"Hmm," said Ygraine thoughtfully, and then gave Flavia a wicked smile that made her insides spin. "Want me to boost you?"

A few moments later, Flavia scrambled on top of a curved, high hedge, panting wildly. She knew she must be bright green in the face from the exertion.

The crow fluttered up to rest primly beside her, and became Ygraine again, fully clothed and looking pleased with herself.

Flavia had spent most of her life working alongside Young Ladies of Quality (including most of her fellow students at the School of Good Wives and God's Mercy, who were training to be governesses because they were Impoverished Ladies of Quality) and in all that time, only Queenie Gloucester had surprised her — she had thought she knew what to expect from a princess. But Ygraine turned out to have gumption. More than a little gumption, Flavia had to admit. Miss Troughton would have been impressed with how soundly the two of them conquered this hedge, and would have been certain to recruit Ygraine for the school hockey team immediately.

"Golly," said Ygraine, breathing hard. "What a sight."

The land of Faerie spiralled out beneath them: all mists and greenery, rivers and mountains. It looked like a watercolour sketch of the world, with several land-marks of different countries spilled on top of each other. There were lagoons, tropical groves, oak forests, gullies and peaks.

Impossibly large; impossibly beautiful. Miniature and enormous at the same time. It hurt the eye to look too closely.

"It really is an island," noted Ygraine. "I thought that was a metaphor. How did Queen Bess ever get them all to agree?"

"I don't know the real story," Flavia admitted. "A trick of some kind? My people..." she paused for a moment. "You know what I am?"

"I'm not blind," scoffed Ygraine, waving a hand at Flavia's green skin.

"My people always said it was unfair," Flavia said staunchly. "That Queen Bess broke some rule of hospitality... I don't know how it happened."

"She must have been brave, my ancestress," mused

Ygraine. "And clever. To trick a whole — well, all the fairies. Every single one of them. And trap them here for centuries."

"They want to break out," Flavia admitted. "I was supposed to help them do it. But I didn't want the children to be hurt."

Ygraine shuddered. "Britannia is at the mercy of enough magic already," she said. "I hate to think... do you hear that?"

Flavia had heard nothing, but Ygraine was up already, scrambling across the top of the uneven hedge. She had lost her boots somewhere, Flavia noticed belatedly. The barefoot princess ran as easily as if she was a fairy herself, leaping from one hedge to another in her full silk gown with ruffled skirt.

Ygraine's hair had fallen loose of its previous arrangement, in dark tangles spiralling down her back, but she still looked as if five minutes with a lady's maid might smarten herself up well enough for Tea with Mother.

Perhaps ten minutes, Flavia mused, given that Ygraine's mother was the Empress of Britannia.

"*Here*," cried Ygraine and became a crow again, swooping between two layers of hedge...

"Wait," Flavia called, and hurried after her.

For the first time since she set foot in the land of Faerie, she felt light. As if there was nothing to worry about at all. As if her burdens were...

As she reached the spot where Ygraine had disappeared, she heard something that dashed an icy chill directly down her back.

It was the sparkling, musical sound of the Queen of Faerie, laughing.

Ygraine

sister of Princess Unity of Bavaria

Orlando and Rinaldo attended my seventeenth birthday ball, exactly as they were supposed to. Both of them danced with me: one waltz each, perfectly proper. They joined in the cheers when my betrothal to Archie Lyonesse was announced, and promptly set off a display of mechanical doves in a heart-shaped formation.

Orlando was no longer Orlando, but I didn't know that yet.

Let's not dwell on it. I still can't think about it without crying.

I'll tell you about Unity.

There were six years between Unity's birth and my own. Most of my sisters ignored my existence, which

181

was hardly a surprise given that they were grown up (or nearly there) before I was old enough to be of interest. Arwenna sometimes played with me when I begged, and Iseult was kind, I think. For the most part, my sisters did not think a scrap about me if I was not in the room.

Only Unity actively despised me.

I shouldn't take it personally. Unity hated everyone. She certainly hated the existence of the Extraordinary and Miraculous Device Brothers.

(If they'd ruined *her* wedding, there would have been blood on the carpet.)

Five years in Bavaria had not made Unity any sweeter when she returned to Britannia for my ball.

"He's not very bright, is he?" she said, appearing like a wicked fairy in the ballet the second that Viscount Lyon left my side to fetch me a glass of ratafia.

Unity wore a waterfall bustle in plum silk with silver trim and so much French lace I was surprised she could lift her arms. She quite left my cream ruffles in the shade; I was unsurprised that she wished to outshine me.

"He's kind," I said sharply.

Unity gave me a look, as if defending my betrothed was a dig at her own marriage. "You won't be happy," she warned. "If you weren't happy being a princess, being a married viscountess won't suit you any better.

Or a duchess, if his father has the good sense to die before your wedding."

"Who says I'm unhappy?"

Unity always cut to the meat of things. Strange how someone who dislikes you can be the person who knows you best. "You've never been happy, Ygraine," she sighed, skewering a pencil into her dance card. "You've always had one foot out the door. It's a terrible look on a princess."

I danced with Orlando, who was handsome and careless as ever.

"Are you well?" I asked when I was able to cut through the surface banter. "I was so worried... is it getting worse? Why all the secrecy? Rinaldo's been like a bear with a sore head."

Orlando spun me perfectly across the room, a gentleman of foreign appearance with pretty eyes and outrageously rumpled hair. Ladies sighed as we went past — the married ladies most of all. They knew trouble when they saw it. "I've no idea what you're on about, your highness. I'm perfectly well."

"But your magic," I pressed. "Orlando, there's something wrong with your magic, and it's hurting you. Don't you remember?"

He plucked a hairpin from my head, transforming it into a buttercup and then tucking it back into the pretty coif of braids and ribbons that my maid had spent hours on. "Nothing wrong with me. Ship-shape and Bristol fashion."

How could he not remember?

~

Archie gave me a grail.

At least, it was a pretty goblet, pale gold and decorated with ornate detail. It was small, like an egg cup, nestled into a bed of padded lilac silk in a polished box.

"That's lovely," I gasped. I'd been expecting something dull for my betrothal gift — a necklace is hard to get excited about when you've watched your mother adorn herself in Crown Jewels for decades.

"It was my grandmother's," said Archie earnestly. "It's a Cornish tradition to give a cup to a new bride, for good luck. And we can drink a toast from it at the wedding," he added, with some measure of awkwardness.

Of course, the taking of love philtres would require a ceremonial cup, and this was as good as any. If we chose not to take philtres, we could use it for wine to toast our good health.

"It's perfect," I promised him.

It would be. I would make sure of it.

~

"What's wrong with Orlando?" I asked Rinaldo as we waltzed, holding each other with perfect correctness. "Why is he forgetting things?"

Rinaldo's face shut down entirely. "I don't want to talk about this."

"Would you prefer we were polite about the weather for the next six minutes?"

"If you can't stomach silence."

I fumed at him for a while, so I suppose he had his silence.

"Why is *she* here?" he asked after a long moment. His eyes were on a lady across the ballroom in an extraordinary gown: bright scarlet silk that did not suit her pale complexion or golden hair, though she was terribly beautiful regardless.

"Isn't everyone here?" I asked. "I don't know her."

"Lady Mortmain."

"The enchantress?" That surprised me. "She might have married a Lord, but I can't see mamma putting someone like her on the guest list."

The only magic endorsed by Queen Isolda was that which could be presented as science of the new age: the ingenious inventions of the Device Brothers passed her approval, but nothing that smacked of the otherworldly.

The beautiful bronze tree that the Devices made me as a birthday gift the year before had already been shipped to a museum because Mama hated the sight of it.

Rinaldo was ignoring me, his eyes on the mysterious Lady Mortmain. She was a widow, I had heard, which made her gown all the more brazen; our family had a long and tormented history with mourning blacks, but crimson on a widow was beyond the pale.

"Be careful what you eat and drink tonight," was all Rinaldo said, before our dance ended.

What would Good Queen Bess do?

She probably wouldn't spend her birthday ball and her first night as a betrothed lady hiding on a balcony behind the supper room, wondering why she couldn't have one sister to really talk to.

Then again, Queen Bess's only sister had not been very nice to her, either.

Early in her reign, Mama commissioned a massive bronze statue of Elizabeth I to be built on the main lawn behind the palace, facing the West Terrace; years later, Papa tweaked the statue with a combination of sparks and mechanical ingenuity so that her eyelids blinked, and her high arrangement of curled hair moved now and then as if caught a breeze.

The Elizabeth Memorial was beautiful and terrifying, much like the queen herself must have been. I often came to look at her, when I was feeling lonely. Not that I had to travel far — Big Bess could be seen from every rear window in the palace.

The ballroom had no balconies, which was one of the elements (along with high windows) which made it so claustrophobic. You had to come out through the dining room to find this particular nook overlooking the lawn; and yet I was easily found.

"There you are!" Archie Lyonesse came sidling through the balcony doors, followed as ever by his discreet valet with a platter of cakes and a jug of lemon water. "You haven't eaten a thing."

"We shouldn't be alone out here," I started to say, because Mr Greenaway did not count as a chaperone.

"Who's alone?" said Orlando, strolling through the doors as the valet withdrew. "Quite the party we have." He was holding a bottle of champagne, still corked.

"You do make friends quickly," I remarked.

"I've asked Mr Device to get me up to scratch," said Archie. "What's what in the palace, how to find my way around, which duchesses not to offend, and the like."

"That one's easy," said Orlando, leaning into Archie like they had been chums for years. "No duchesses. Don't offend a single duchess or you'll be out on your ear."

I wished Archie wasn't here. How was I to find out what was wrong with Orlando with a viscount in our way?

Mindful of Rinaldo's warning, I refused the cakes but accepted a glass of the champagne, because I had watched Orlando open it. It should be safe.

Assuming that this was Orlando. Now that the thought occurred to me, I found myself examining every detail. Did his hair flop about with its usual defiance of gravity? Were the studs of his collar too tightly pressed? Had his fingernails always looked like that?

"Don't you think so, your highness?" asked Archie, pink in the face and eager to please.

"That sounds lovely," I murmured, which must have been the right answer, for he did not look confused — though Orlando gave me a quick, darting look. I had not fooled him.

"Goodness, Ygraine, are you trying to spark a scandal?" declared Unity, steering her massive plum bustle through the balcony doors to break up our cosy gathering.

The gentlemen made their bows and left out of politeness, leaving me at the utter mercy of my sister.

"You really should wait until you're married before you thread more men on your string," she said from pure cattiness.

"Why did you come?" I snapped back. "You don't like me. You've never liked me. Is Bavaria so dull that you'll take any excuse to ride over the mountains and make my life a misery?"

Unity gave me a sharp, mocking look. "Let's not pretend I'm the one making you miserable," she purred. "Did dear Arwenna bother to stir herself all the miles from *Dorset* to make an appearance? What a trial her travel itinerary must be."

"She's with child," I muttered. "Probably." My mother had utilised at least three confusing metaphors when explaining Arwenna's absence, so I assumed that was the case.

"Or she's obsessively in love with her husband because she took one of those horrid little potions, and barely thinks about us any more," Unity sniped back.

That had more truth to it than I liked to admit.

Perhaps there would be a peace in it, to take the potion. Only loving one person, caring what *one* person thought in all the world, instead of constantly having to juggle the potential disapproval of mother, sisters, and the nation.

The idea was starting to appeal.

"Then there's our mother," sighed Unity, almost human for a moment. "Who doesn't even have that as an excuse for her disinterest." She scowled at me, toying at the cakes on the tray. "Doesn't it bother you that they've set you up to be the next Iseult? They're binding you to a Lyonesse, the ballad writes itself."

"Wait," I blurted as Unity seized the largest, prettiest cake and bit into it. "Don't —"

Everything that came next happened quickly, and all at once.

We learned later that the cake had been dosed with a love philtre, a powerful one. We never found out who did it.

Archie Lyonesse and his valet were questioned at length, but Mr Greenaway claimed to have lifted the plate directly from the shared supper table. A rare and highly illegal truth philtre was utilised, to be sure of the evidence taken from Viscount Lyon, his valet, and even Orlando.

Did Rinaldo's Lady Mortmain do the deed? I never found out whether she was even suspected — she left the party long before the incident.

That's how they always referred to it, afterwards. The incident.

~

What happened is this:

When she bit into the cake, Unity received a startlingly high and near-toxic dose of a love philtre. With no convenient humans within her line of sight, she fell instantly in love with the statue of Good Queen Bess, resplendent on the lawn.

Before I could stop her, she hurled herself off the balcony to be with the object of her affection.

We were two floors up: she would surely have died if she fell any further. From her scream as she landed, I thought for a moment she had. Instead, Unity broke an ankle, cracked a rib and still managed to drag herself to the plinth, trailing blood along the paving stones of the West Terrace.

The whole scene was terrifying. She was wild-eyed, utterly lacking in any control.

By the time Orlando and I made it down the Grand Staircase to the garden, we had to elbow our way through a crowd of party guests who had been out there taking the air; I wasn't the only one who found the ballroom stifling.

So many witnesses to see the Princess of Bavaria, bloodstained and lovelorn, tearing off half her gown in wild-eyed lust as she professed her amour to a giant statue. There was no hushing this up.

Rinaldo, reaching the scene only a little behind us, produced a dose of Love-Me-Not. Unity, clinging wildly to Big Bess, refused to touch any philtre that came from his hand. She shouted to the crowd that he was trying to murder her.

It was Mama, in the end, emerging white-lipped and straight-backed into the terrible scene, who administered the antidote to her daughter and wrapped her in a cloak before having her carried inside by a footman.

I had tried to help and been of no use at all; my pale silk gown was now stained with my sister's blood.

Unity left for Bavaria three days later and never returned to Britannia, claiming she could not survive the humiliation. I never saw her again.

Mama tried to keep an eye on Unity's recovery from a distance, but everything came through her maid, or her husband. We heard she suffered from blood poisoning, and later a 'melancholic malaise.'

Concerned, Mama sent a cohort of physicians, who at least reported back detailed information about Unity's health and state of mind, though the news was never good.

A year after the ball, we heard that the Bavarian Royal Family had sent Unity to some asylum in the mountains. Mama's chief physician approved of the move, but shortly thereafter wrote to inform her that her daughter had passed away.

Of a chill, according to official reports.

People do die of chills, of course. It happens every day. Even young, healthy women who are not with child. Even princesses.

And yet.

To this day, Mama is certain it was the cake that killed Unity. I can't help but believe the same.

No one has ever told me so to my face, but I am perfectly certain that the cake was meant for me.

Queens in Houses *by William Morris* (1882) *is said to be the only poetic sequence in the English language which also qualifies as a Gothic novel. His portrayal of Tanaquil Gloriana Queen of All Fae as a terrifying girl-child was supposedly based on the first-hand account of a survivor of the* 1878 *Siege of Buckingham Palace.*

However, in 1972, *Tipcham and Mead uncovered an archived letter from* 1908 *in which Jane Morris writes to her good friend the Countess of Carlisle claiming that the romantic and tragic fervour we see so vividly in her husband's literary masterwork "owed more to a weekend drinking absinthe while reading John Keats than any genuine source material."*

— Benedetta West, "Popular Literary
Interpretations of the Siege of
Miracles," *Bradamante* journal, pp
85-86, 1996

Chapter 9

In Which a Duchess and a Governess Take Tea with the Queen

Surrounded by the eerie sound of her mother's laughter, Flavia leaned over the edge of the maze wall and tumbled on to the grass. She found herself in an exquisite grove, lush with bright fruit and flowers. She was not familiar with these types of trees, with trunks twisted into elaborate shapes, though the scent of the air reminded her of somewhere she had been recently.

The air was hot and sticky, like walking through a greenhouse.

It was all a little too perfect, for Faerie. Too civilised. Every plant was trimmed expertly, as if gardeners had been at work. Symmetrical stone archways led back into the hedge maze.

A pathway of pebbles. Since when did Faerie lay paths of stone?

Ygraine stood there, red in the face and clearly

over-heated in her blue ruffled walking dress. "Will you look at this?" she demanded, gesticulating wildly. "Himalayan walnut! Betel nut palm, bamboo, banyan, mango!" She picked the lush, large fruit from a knobbled spine of a branch. "*Mango*, Miss Wednesday."

Flavia was not entirely sure what emotional reaction a mango was supposed to inspire in her. "How dare they," she ventured.

"It's not just the plants, it's the path." Ygraine gestured at a winding stone path.

"I've been wondering about that," said Flavia.

"It's the same path," Ygraine raged. "The same trees, the same flowers. There's a lotus pond. This isn't *just* an Indian garden. It's the exact Indian garden that my mother commissioned for the grounds of Buckingham Palace."

Oh, that wasn't good. "She's been taking an interest in the outside world," said Flavia worriedly. "She must have been spying on Buckingham Palace."

Flavia knew of two other houses in which the Queen of Faerie had taken a particular interest — Gloucester Worth, and 12 Actaeon Place. It hadn't worked out well for the people who lived in those houses.

Ygraine gave her a startled look. "Who? Who did this?"

"My mother." Flavia's voice was heavy enough that she must surely convey the dread with which she contemplated the reunion. "She's dangerous."

Ygraine's face softened. "Mine too," she admitted. "Of course, mine is a queen, which makes things difficult..."

Flavia let out a yelp of a laugh. "Yes," she said wildly. "Same here."

A slow look of realisation came over the face of the princess, as she remembered where they were. "You're not..."

"I am."

"Did you not think to mention you were the daughter of the Queen of Faerie?"

"It's not exactly a boast," Flavia retorted. "More of a millstone around my neck. If my mother has the Gloucester children already, she will have her way. She doesn't just want to lead the fairies back to Britannia. She has plans for when they get there."

"Invade and colonise," Ygraine said crisply. "If she's been watching the way my mother works, I have no doubt that her plans are to invade and colonise."

Flavia opened her mouth to say more, but Ygraine washed out before her eyes, like a cup of tea thrown over a watercolour painting. Colours bled and twisted in the air, and the entire warm hillside and Indian garden melted into a mist that smelled of sandwiches and Earl Grey.

"Oh," said Flavia, swaying on her feet.

Ygraine was still here. She looked determined, too, and solid. Her cheeks were rosy, her teeth gritted. She reached out and took Flavia's hand — the one still made of flesh. "Be strong," she murmured. "We'll get through this."

"And here you both are," said a warm, inviting voice. "Please join me for tea."

One of the stone arches widened to be more welcoming. Flowers burst into bloom around it. Holding Ygraine's hand as if it was the only thing tethering her to the ground, Flavia walked through.

The trees and flowers fell away behind them, like they had been folded up into a box full of handkerchiefs. Flavia and Ygraine now stood inside a stone gazebo identical to the one in Buckingham Palace... but twice as large.

Tanaquil Gloriana, Queen of Faerie, sat at a delicate table covered in all the fixings for high tea, her long fingers wrapped around the handle of a porcelain teapot.

There were three chairs.

Gloriana's true face was familiar, though her body was not — this was perfectly usual, as Flavia's mother rarely looked the same twice apart from her mask. Her mask was made of braided branches, budding with blossom. It looked as fresh as ever, though the mask and its owner were hundreds, perhaps thousands of years old.

(Fairies did not like to count.)

The queen's hair was high and golden in curls, an arrangement taken directly from the fashion sketches of *The Lady*. She wore gentleman's clothes, of all things, though her current body was more bosomy than usual, squeezed into breeches, low-cut shirt and a tailored waistcoat, all woven from grasses. The effect was sensual and entirely alien: not quite human, not quite fey. (Better at least than when the Queen liked to playact at being a child, which Flavia had always found disturbing.) Her golden curls were topped off with a prim top hat decorated with buttercups, like she'd just strolled in from Rotten Row by way of Covent Garden.

Ygraine stared, as if she did not know whether to be horrified or intrigued by this bizarre, cutting edge fashion.

Everything Tanaquil Gloriana did was a performance: Flavia was not certain which of them was the intended audience for this particular show.

"Sit, please," said the Queen of Faerie, pouring green liquid into perfect cups. "Eat something. You must be in need of refreshments."

Ygraine moved first, the palace etiquette kicking in. "Thank you so much," she said nicely, dropping into a chair and pulling Flavia to do the same. They were still holding hands. "I won't eat, if you don't mind. I distrust tiny cakes."

"Do you like my gazebo?" the Queen asked, her bright green eyes locked on Flavia from behind her mask. "I miss walls," she went on in a warm voice. "Walls and cake were two things I liked best about that Other Place, the mortal realm. I don't miss the clothes," she added, with a pitying look at Flavia's petticoat. "It was worse in my day — velvet layers, stiff bodices, and those scratchy ruffs which I see are back in fashion, more's the pity. Mortal women lurched from room to room like four-poster beds, tucking cloves and dried oranges into every crevice rather than risk the healthful consequences of a bath. Still. This century isn't a great improvement. The crinoline continues to hang on, and that bustle business is absurd." She gave Ygraine a brief, sniffing glance. "Haven't you managed to bring bloomers into the common fashion yet?"

"Me personally?" said the princess.

"You lead the fashions, do you not, Princess Ygraine?" the Queen said mildly.

Flavia shivered at that. Of course, her mother knew who Ygraine was. It felt dangerous. She tried to release Ygraine's hand from under the table, but the princess hung on ruthlessly.

"Did you bring us here to chat about frocks?" Flavia asked in a resentful mutter.

"Drink your tea and sit straight," said her mother. "We're playing at ladies."

Flavia eyed the teacup. It looked milky, but when she raised it to her lips all she could smell was rosehips and sugar. "Good try," she observed, putting the cup down again.

Her mother waved an airy hand, as if only the look of the thing mattered.

"Where did you get this cup?" Ygraine asked in an odd voice.

Flavia glanced over and saw that the princess's teacup was no longer china, but a tiny silver goblet, covered in an exquisite honeycomb pattern and studded with jewelled bees.

"I wanted you to feel at home," said Queen Gloriana in a soothing voice. "Will you drink?"

"I'm not thirsty," said Ygraine, but her hand stayed curled around the cup.

Flavia was overwhelmed by a memory: a different tea table, and a dizzy sensation of wanting to speak nothing but the truth. She looked back to her mother, peering around the familiar mask or "true face" to the physical reality beneath. "Are you wearing Lady Mortmain's body?" she demanded.

Ygraine dropped the silver cup. Tea splashed across the tablecloth. "What?"

"What does it matter whose body I wear?" asked the Queen with a sigh.

"How long?" Flavia growled.

"Mind your manners, Flaxenseed. Address me with respect." Her mother's cruel smile was visible beneath the twisted branches of her mask. "You have another arm to lose."

Flavia banged her cup and saucer down on the table and stood up, finally pulling her hand out of Ygraine's. "How long have you been walking around inside that enchantress?"

"You suspected I had a spy in her household, did you not?" smirked her mother, toying with a pocket on the grass waistcoat. "This woman has been attempting to break through to Faerie — to steal my power for herself — since she was nine years old. I drop in on her from time to time, to make sure she isn't getting too big for her... britches." She shifted slightly in her chair and gave a smirk that was the same no matter what body she wore.

"Was it you who drugged me at the tea table?" Flavia demanded. "Was it you who —" But of course, *of course* it had been her mother who managed that explosion in the attic. It was no coincidence that the philtres and the brass fountain melded together in exactly the right way to bring Lady Mortmain and the children here...

"Now you're thinking," said the Queen of Faerie, sounding approving.

"Why did you need her here? The children, you needed the children, but why do you need this woman?"

"It's charming that you think I'm going to answer your questions." Her mother shuddered for a moment, and lifted her head a little higher, wetting her lips. Her eyes were suddenly bright blue. "She wants to punish me," she said in a different voice. The real Lady Mortmain. "She wants me to witness her triumph."

"Where are the children?" Flavia asked immediately. "What has she done with them?

Lady Mortmain started to speak, but her body

twitched and her eyes became green again. "None of that," the Queen said smoothly. "*Bad* hostess."

"What do you want with Rinaldo Device?" Flavia asked abruptly. It hadn't been the question at the forefront of her mind, but as soon as it occurred to her, she found that she desperately needed the answer.

The branch-and-blossom mask stretched into a smile. "Why," said her mother. "He's going to build me a gate, and his brother will bring it to life."

And let it run with blood, Flavia supposed. *Queenie and Dash's blood.* "You're a monster."

"Your words are so small," said her mother. "It is a wonder you bother to let them fall out of your mouth. The important thing is that you kept our bargain after all. The Gloucester children are mine."

Ygraine gave Flavia a startled look.

"I did not keep our bargain," Flavia insisted.

"I accept your gift," the Queen said serenely.

Her head twitched slightly, as if Lady Mortmain was struggling to the surface once more.

Flavia was sick of this, so sick of tiptoeing around her mother's demands in order to please her. *Nothing I ever do will be good enough.* "They were not my gift," she said with slow, careful enunciation.

The mask shuddered on the Faerie Queen's face, and fell away, revealing a blazingly furious Lady Mortmain, with bags of exhaustion under her bright blue eyes.

"They were my gift," the enchantress declared. She

leaped to her feet, addressing the empty air. "I gave my niece and nephew to you! I was supposed to be rewarded."

Flavia lost what remained of her temper. "You're as bad as each other!" she shouted. "What kind of creatures are you? You're their aunt, you should be protecting them," she spat at Lady Mortmain, who lifted her chin. "And you —" Where to even direct her words? "You're supposed to be my mother," Flavia said bitterly.

The enchantress took a deep breath and picked up the mask as if she was one of Rinaldo and Orlando's automata. Stiffly, she placed back on her face as Tanaquil Gloriana took over once again.

Ygraine had moved out of the way, the silver goblet still clutched in her hands as she backed up against the temple wall. Flavia could only hope that she made the sensible decision to *run*.

"What is a mother, compared to a Queen?" said Gloriana, stretching the mortal body to be taller, wider, grander. She had little respect for mortal flesh, not being used to its restrictions. "What makes you think you are worthy of my attention, Flaxenseed, merely because I set you free upon the world? You refused the job for which I created you!"

"What is a mother?" Flavia repeated quietly. "What is a *Queen*? What is the point of you, if you deal in nothing but blood and misery? What is the point of unleashing your empty creatures of magic and greenwood on the mortal world? What would you even do with it?"

Her mother tilted her head thoughtfully. "I would eat the mortal empire alive," she said. "What did you think I was going to do?"

~

The House of Flowers was no longer a prison. Rinaldo's magic had taken it over entirely, bleeding fine bronze wires through the veins of the trunks and branches that formed the various rooms and doors and lintels.

He had stretched the metal thin, thinner than any he had worked with before, but it had warmed in response to his magic, and lent him strength in return.

When in doubt, his magic always defaulted to the shape of a man, whether he was building an automaton to entertain villagers, or a creature of teaspoons to entertain a friend.

He had not quite gone that far in this instance: but he had built a strong pair of legs out of tree roots and moss, which lifted the house in the air high above the grasping, prodding fingers of the pixys and goblins.

No one had stopped him. The queen of this country must be distracted elsewhere, to have let two of her prizes escape in such away.

Queenie clung to the walls of a parlour made from braided daffodils and buttercups, her face frozen into a sort of grimace as if she did not know whether to be afraid, or furious, or triumphant.

"Do you know what you're doing?" she asked him, only once.

"Miracles, I can manage," said Rinaldo, gritting his teeth as he learned to steer this new shambling, top-heavy house on legs. "I've no idea how to find your brother, or the others." He had not admitted to her yet that last time he saw young Dashmond, he was being worn by a particularly homicidal fairy with silver eyes.

There was a sound, like the grinding of gears inside a complex clock. A blur of yellow appeared in one of the windows. The cat who had once been the young Duke of Cornwall glared at them both and hawked up a few copper wires.

"Where were you an hour ago?" Rinaldo demanded.

The cat turned his back and rather deliberately pointed his nose in a specific direction.

"I mean," said Queenie thoughtfully. "We don't have any better ideas?"

Now they strode over the hills and valleys of this strange and glorious land, lurching on tree-root legs as they made their journey. Every now and then, Cornwall would cough or yowl to get Rinaldo's attention and point with his nose.

"I don't know that you have to keep doing that," said Queenie, scratching the cat under his chin. "We're all going in the same direction."

205

They were making their way across a wide wild-flower meadow large enough to hold a city. Rinaldo had been concentrating on making each step of the walking house safely, but now he looked up he saw not only more sky than he had ever seen in his life, but also a mass of running, tumbling, flying creatures all around them.

There was a hill up ahead crowned with dark, tall green hedges, and every fairy in the land was heading right for it. As were they.

Cornwall made no objection as Rinaldo steered the House of Flowers directly to the hill swarming with fairy creatures, and finally let go of the magic so that the legs folded up underneath the house, settling in on to the dirt once more.

"What are you waiting for?" demanded Queenie.

Rinaldo had not realised how exhausted he was until he stopped. Now he could not imagine getting started again. "I don't think it goes up hills," he managed.

Queenie snorted with more scorn than he'd ever heard from an audience, even when they were hurling kitchen scraps.

The cat let out an almighty screech. All the fur on his back stood up straight.

He was a miraculous creation all right, however accidental his transformation had been.

Queenie leaned out of one of the windows, having loosened the bars of thorn and thistle. "Is that..." she said. "It looks like her. Right out of the fashion sketches in *The Lady*!"

"What?" Rinaldo unwound the last connections between himself and the House of Flowers and joined her at the window. "Who is it?"

"It's the princess," reported Queenie. "The youngest princess. She's always been my favourite, because she looks so cross when they take her picture for the newspapers."

Rinaldo let out a wheeze like he had been punched in the chest. It was *Ygraine*. The new Duchess of Cornwall and Land's End (and Viscountess Lyon and probably other titles as well), in a fashionable blue gown still mostly holding together. As the fairies and all the little grasping creatures swarmed up the hill towards whatever was happening up there, Ygraine came down against the flow, shoving and slapping at any hands, feet or wings that got in her way.

She looked angry and out of breath. Rinaldo was wildly confused to see her here.

The House of Flowers obeyed him now, so he barely had to push on the large arched door before it gave way under his fingers, letting him scramble to the grass. He ran up the hill, tripping over goblins as he went. "Ygraine!"

Her head jerked up as she heard him, and then suddenly she was a crow, up the air, black wings flapping wildly.

She had never shown any signs of magic. Her

mother would have found a way to get her out of the palace much earlier if that was the case. Transformation. Where had that ability come from?

The bird swooped down on him, beak first, and then Ygraine was in his arms, swaying woozily and laughing into his neck like they had just been performing the most elaborate waltz.

(They had waltzed at her birthday ball, only a few hours before that awful incident with her sister. She was cross at him, and suspicious, but they had still danced together beautifully, as they always did. They had learned together, after all.)

"What are you doing?" Rinaldo asked in astonishment.

Ygraine gave him a wild smack about the shoulder, though the blow had little strength to it. There was a rosy pink to her cheeks and a light in her eyes that he had not seen in years. "You bastard. You turned my husband into a *cat*."

That was true, though a lot of things had happened since then.

"How are you here?" Rinaldo demanded.

"I came with Orlando, of course. And Miss Wednesday." Ygraine patted her dark curls as if there was any way she could possibly tidy them. She looked like she had been pulled through a hedge backwards. "We need to go back and help her. She's absolutely right, her mother is much scarier than mine. I wouldn't have thought it possible."

Rinaldo frowned. "Where's Orlando, if not with Miss Wednesday?"

"Is my brother with her?" Queenie yelled through a window. "Sorry I can't curtsey, but I don't believe in it!"

"Neither do I," Ygraine called back in response. "You must be Miss Gloucester. I've been looking forward to meeting you. I'm afraid I haven't seen your brother."

Silver eyes and a mocking smile. Rinaldo pushed that thought quickly out of his head. "We'll get Flavia first," he decided.

Ygraine frowned. "No, wait. You can't go anywhere near the Faerie Queen, Rinaldo. You're essential to her plan."

Rinaldo had assumed he was pulled here by accident, after the explosion in the attic. "What does she want with me?"

"Something about building a gate."

Rinaldo's heart sank, as he remembered the bronze fountain at Number 12, Actaeon Place. "I'm not taking commissions at this time," he muttered.

"It's not the Solstice yet," said Queenie, climbing out of her window and dropping to the grass like she had been doing such things her whole life. "I'd been counting the days before we ended up here."

Ygraine fumbled in her dress and brought out a very familiar looking clockwork beetle. "Here," she said, shoving it at Rinaldo. "You should use this to get yourself and the children home. It's contaminated with something that might turn you into a bird but honestly it hasn't been much of a hindrance."

Rinaldo laughed. It was strangely good to see her again, even if it was under the direst circumstances. "Ygraine. I'm not abandoning you in a magical kingdom with no way home."

"Why not? I'll be all right. Orlando is around here somewhere. And it's not like my mother can get any more annoyed at you. You need to go. Or all the Fairy Queen's plans will go exactly as she wants, and the fairies will return to Britannia and... they'll eat us alive. Like Britannia has eaten the world."

Rinaldo shook his head. "Rescuing Queenie won't stop the Queen's plans if Dash is still running around the Isle of Faerie." *Controlled by a monster.*

"I don't plan to abandon my brother," Queenie put in sharply.

"I never thought you would," Rinaldo assured her. He was going to have to break it to her about her brother's current predicament. As soon as he could find the words.

A gate. What made the Queen of the Faerie think Rinaldo would work for her? (Not that Lady Mortmain had exactly given him a choice about the fountain.)

"Perhaps the cat can find Dash," said Queenie, staring openly at the dishevelled princess. "He did a good job of finding you."

"Cat," murmured Ygraine, looking up into the

House of Flowers. Her eyes softened as she recognised the bright yellow cat perching warily on a window ledge. "Oh," she said in a sigh. "There you are. Hello, Archie."

Archibalt Lyonesse, the Duke of Cornwall and Land's End, trapped in the form of a yellow cat, nodded his head gracefully to his wife.

Ygraine

Queen of Cups

I dreamed of my wedding the night before. Every bride does, I suppose.

I was sitting at the high table in the state dining room, my green dress adorned with orange blossom. Archie at my side, though everyone called him Cornwall these days — his father had, as Unity predicted, died before the wedding, so I was to marry a duke, not a viscount. Archie looked presentable enough in his scarlet cavalry uniform, though no one has ever needed that much yellow braid to demonstrate they are wearing formal attire.

Everyone ate and drank and made merry.

I was thirsty.

There were cups everywhere: teacups, wine glasses, and silver goblets. Every time I reached for one, someone else would snatch it away.

I rose in my long dress and made my way down the

aisle between tables, grasping at cup after cup, never managing to hold one for more than a moment.

Finally, I saw it. The tiny gold goblet that Archie had given me as a betrothal gift, before he was Cornwall and Land's End, before Unity died, before I learned the truth about Orlando.

It rested on a velvet cushion, and I knew why. This was the philtre that would change my life.

Thirst scraped my throat raw. "If I drink," I said. "Will you drink too?"

No one answered me.

I lifted the cup, held it to my lips... and dust poured into my mouth. I coughed and flung the cup away...

There's another dream I've had my whole life — details change, but it's basically the same every time. I'm sitting in a room made of stone, across the tea table from a queen. Not Mama, though I suppose all queens in dreams probably represent my mother.

She looks more like the queen on a chess board, all pale and featureless. Stern like the queen on a deck of cards. Remorseless, like...

Well, yes. Mama.

The table between us is covered in grails, like something out of the chivalric myths.

"Let us play cup or crown," says the queen, and

moves the cups around, one after the other. "Which one is empty?"

It's not much of a game. "They're all empty."

"Look closer."

I reach into the sea of cups and pull out a goblet that feels familiar. It has the same detailed crest as the cup Archie gave me, but it is larger, fitting my hand perfectly. I can't tell if it is silver or gold — sometimes it is one, sometimes the other. This grail, *my* grail is full to the brim with a sweet cordial.

I drink, and with every mouthful I feel good and warm. The pale queen asks me questions about my life, all our stories.

I spill them out for her: every secret from Buckingham Palace. I talk about my father, my uncle, my sisters and their husbands. I tell her about the Miraculous and Extraordinary Device Brothers, all the fun we had together, how I hated them and then I loved them, and they broke my heart.

I talk about my mother, and how she never cared about me except as a piece on the board.

As I talk, and sip from the gold-and-silver grail, the pale queen moves the cups in an ever-changing pattern until I am dizzy. I cannot see her clearly any more, all I hear are the words until I run out and then all is silence.

Finally, I swallow the last sip from the cup.

The queen is gone.

I am alone in the garden.

As I place the grail back on the table, I hear a voice in my ear, all crisp and commanding like one of my old governesses.

She says: "You're the queen now, Ygraine. Start acting like it!"

I never knew who that voice belonged to, until now.

It's your voice, Flavia.

We foot it all the night,
    Weaving olden dances,
    Mingling hands and mingling glances
    Till the moon has taken flight;
    To and fro we leap
    And chase the frothy bubbles.

While the world is full of troubles
    And is anxious in its sleep.
    Come away, O human child!
    To the woods and waters wild
    With a fairy, hand in hand,
    For the world's more full of weeping than
you can understand.

— W.B. Yeats, *The Stolen Child*, 1889

Chapter 10

In Which Fairies Prepare Themselves to Journey to a Foreign Country

Flavia was not a prisoner.

If anything, she was a guest in her mother's court. And this was the court now. It could not be mistaken for anything else.

The scenery had shifted about like someone was arranging new backgrounds for a paper theatre. The stone gazebo opened up to reveal a wide courtyard, surrounded by greenery.

The remaining wall of the gazebo was taller, shaped into elegant turrets like the paper-cut illustrations of a fairy tale. A false castle: a parody of the real thing.

The exotic Indian trees had doubled in size, towering over them all with their sweet mangoes and strong flowers. But there were more familiar Britannian trees mixed up in them: oaks and alders, birches and willows.

Some trees burst forth with flowers, while others hung heavy with fruit. One oak tree at the back dropped acorns and leaves in a slow ritual until the branches were stripped winter-bare, then popped spring blossom from every twig and started the process all over again.

This was what I always wanted, Flavia reminded herself. To sit at her mother's side, to be accepted by her court. Daughter of the Faerie Queen. It felt like such a cruel joke.

Tanaquil Gloriana, still wearing her grassy gentleman's attire and the body of Lady Mortmain, lounged in a basket chair woven with willow fronds. Her top hat had become a golden crown, tall and ringed with spikes. From behind her mask of branches, she watched with intense eyes as the fairies of her court arrived in all their finery.

Flavia recognised many of them: the Queen's favourite creatures, pushed into position at the front of the crowd. Tallow-wisp and Nightwhisper, Borage and Meadowsweet, Dandelion and Sweet-pease. They had danced, all those nights when Flavia visited in her dreams. Sometimes they had even extended their elegant hands to invite her to join them. She had loved them then, though she knew most were humouring her, to please their queen. Many laughed at her — to her face as often as they did behind her back.

(Only Quicksilver acted like she was really Flavia's friend, and that had been the worst lie of all.)

Now, the court gathered around the leafy court-yard on top of the hill, garbed like their queen in strange approximations of 'mortal clothes.'

Dandelion, a cocky fellow who had often tried to steal a kiss from Flavia, wore a tailcoat of feathers and clover leaf with absolutely nothing beneath it. Somehow this made his nudity more disturbing than if he had not worn the coat.

Meadowsweet wore a ruff made of soft rose petals, and a delicate gown that would not look out of place among the sketches of Princess Ygraine's favourite fashions, except that every inch of it from the corseted bustier to the spilling flounces of the skirt and French lace trim was sculpted from the same cobwebs as Meadowsweet's true face.

Tallow-wisp wore a whole crinolette made from climbing roses, which made it impossible for him to sit down.

Borage was dressed in something like footman's livery, covered in violets from head to toe. "Names," she cried, clapping her hands. "We will need lady and gentleman names, when we go among the mortals. It's only right and proper. I shall be... Crystal Palace!"

"I shall be Lilliput," said Meadowsweet, shoving her aside. "Children in the park read it from a book and I thought it was so pretty!"

"Edgar Phillips," said Dandelion, with a dramatic bow. "Sir Edgar Phillips, Baronet."

Flavia did not dare say that this was already the

name of a mortal gentleman who had come to dinner with Lady Mortmain earlier this month.

"Katharina!" cried Sweet-pease, who wore foxglove boots, a matching top hat and the light, layered crinoline skirts of a ballerina on the stage. "Or Marmaduke," she added, dancing in circles so her skirt billowed up and out. "Katherina Marmaduke the Third. Maybe the Fourth, too!"

"I want to be Marmaduke," argued Tallow-wisp, and the two of them fought each other lazily, like cats swiping at each other.

"Children in the park," murmured Flavia under her breath.

Her mother gave her a triumphant look. "There are many ways to watch the world. How else to prepare for our return? The Serpentine is my favourite lake, so conveniently right at the heart of Hyde Park. But there are bodies of water all over Britannia that serve our purpose..." She clapped her hands, surveying the court of fairies as they squabbled about names and greatcoats and whether or not footwear was required among the mortals. "Where is my Quicksilver?"

Flavia caught her breath.

The sea of fairies parted, and an amber fox trotted into the court, transforming as he went into a small boy in pyjamas, striding towards the Queen with all the confidence of a Member of Parliament. He bowed in a grandiose manner, then curtseyed with even more precision. As he straightened up, his eyes glowed silver.

Quicksilver, Flavia's friend and lover, murderer of perfectly nice cooks, had hold of Dash Gloucester's body. It was obscene.

"Don't think I forgive easily, my queen," said the fairy through the mouth of the boy.

"Oh dear," laughed Gloriana. "Have I done something to offend, shining one?"

"You broke my body," said the Hand of the Queen, in a voice sticky with honey. "I have done nothing but serve you, and you tried to destroy me."

The other fairies whispered among each other, clearly worried by what they had heard.

"Nonsense, beloved," said Gloriana. "Look at you, so young and strong. Thriving. And you have brought me my boy."

Quicksilver laughed, borrowing Dashmond's careless giggle. "No, my queen. I'm keeping this one."

"Indeed," said Gloriana, her tone turning to ice. "You think so?"

"These feeble wretches think they can play mortal and be accepted in that other world," said Quicksilver, waving a hand. "Let them have their games, if they can keep it up. I want to do it for real. I can ride this boy to Eton and Cambridge. Take up a seat in the House of Lords. Build a career as the greatest magician ever to walk among them. And you are going to let me do exactly that."

Flavia had never seen these two at odds before: Quicksilver had teased and rebelled, but always stood at her Queen's side. The court of the fey were just as alarmed, their eyes huge as they watched the exchange.

"And why should I do that?" said the Queen of the Fairies.

"Because," said Quicksilver-in-the-body-of-Dashmond. "I can supply all the Gloucester blood you could possibly need." She made a gesture, and the fairy crowd parted again as a mighty mass of vines and thorns and brambles surged through them, landing in a mess of earth and roots and yes, blood at the feet of the queen.

The Honourable Perrault Gloucester, second son of the Earl of Shuttlesworth, was caught in the mass of thorns, his body twisted and wrecked. He breathed roughly, his eyes closed and his spectacles long gone. His skin was bruised and scratched all over. But he breathed. Still alive.

The Queen of the Fairies smiled suddenly, as if the sun had come up to light her face. She clapped merrily, rewarding Quicksilver for the gift. "Delightful!" she sang. "Perfect. Now we only need a magician to build our gate."

"Rinaldo won't do it," Flavia said quietly. "He won't betray his whole people, his *country*."

The Queen of the Fairies shrugged, as if this was of no matter. "He has a brother, does he not? One Device is as good as another."

"It's all gone quiet," said Ygraine, her eyes on the fairy hill.

It felt as if every running, flying, dancing creature in this land had poured up the slopes before their eyes, but now they were all — up there, Rinaldo supposed. Hidden from sight by the thick foliage and green hedges.

The Isle of Faerie was still around them, as if it was already empty.

What if they've already gone? It was a wild thought, if impossible. He hadn't built a gate for the Queen of Faerie. Who else could have done such a thing?

"What do you think they're doing up there?" asked Queenie. She sat despondently on the steps of the House of Flowers. The young girl had attempted to coax Cornwall on to her lap, but the yellow cat looked horrified at the very suggestion.

Ygraine bit her lip. "Miss Wednesday is the queen's daughter," she ventured. "She shouldn't be in too much danger, should she?"

"Of course, she's in danger," broke in a new voice — the most important voice in Rinaldo's life. "That's why we're going to rescue her."

Orlando Device came strolling around the side of the House of Flowers as if he had only been gone five minutes. Rinaldo stared at him, not quite able to take in that he was here.

His brother's gaze held his for a brief moment, like cold iron.

Rinaldo felt his stomach fall out from under him. *He knows.* How could Orlando have possibly found out the truth? His eyes flicked to Ygraine, who avoided his gaze.

"Mr Device!" Queenie cried out with delight. "Are you here to help us rescue my brother?"

"In a manner of speaking," said Orlando. You had to know him very well to hear anything but pure charm in his voice — Rinaldo knew him like he knew his own breath, and he could hear the effort Orlando was making to appear his usual self. Orlando bowed his head: his hair was more of a wreck than usual, though his suit was still in one piece. "If I had my hat, Miss Gloucester, I would doff it."

"Smooth as ever," said Ygraine, still keeping her gaze turned away from Rinaldo. "What's your plan, Orlando? We've all got into such a muddle."

"Ah, yes," said Orlando, his smile warming in the sunshine. "I do have a plan. And the good news is, I've fixed my magic."

No no no no no, Rinaldo thought.

"Was it broken?" Queenie asked, all innocence.

"It was!" said Orlando, still sounding rather chipper. "You see, I thought a wicked lady stole it, but she only put a compulsion on me to make me think my magic didn't work any more. And it lasted rather longer than it should... because there were so many other memory charms and strange magics wrapped up in my system, they all got somewhat tangled." He shot Rinaldo another brief look but did not linger. "I can see why the fairies like this island. So refreshing. A chance to reset and cleanse. They should offer it to mortals as a magical holiday, to pop over and take the waters for their health."

"Orlando," Rinaldo said in a low voice "Can we speak in private?"

Ygraine bit her lip, glancing between the two of them.

"No time, no time!" said Orlando, gesturing for Queenie to head inside the House of Flowers. "We have to move quickly if this is going to work."

Queenie and Cornwall both headed inside obediently.

"What did you do?" Rinaldo whispered to Ygraine.

"It wasn't my fault," she hissed back, and hurried after the others.

Rinaldo's own magic settled happily around him as he set foot back inside the House of Flowers. The vessel might be built and reshaped from the most chaotic magic he had ever worked with, but its thin bronze veins sustained him.

"Marvellous," said Orlando, hands caressing the walls. "I do love your work, professor, as always. This will be *perfect*."

"I don't know what you —" Rinaldo started to say,

but the House of Flowers shuddered into life, the legs unbending to raise them back into the air.

He had not done that. "What are you doing?"

"Your mistake," Orlando said lightly, "Was not being more suspicious that they gave you a knife. Honestly. I thought you were the practical one. And you've used so much of your magic — pouring it into this beautiful house. Don't you have an ounce of self-preservation?" He did meet his brother's eyes then, with an icy gaze. "But that's Rinaldo Device for you. Always worrying about everyone else. Never looking after yourself."

"What's happening?" Queenie asked. Ygraine tried to give her a comforting pat on the shoulder, but she shook her off. "I'm not a child. What's wrong with him?"

"Nothing's wrong, dear," said Orlando brightly. "Everything is marvellous. Might want to hold on."

The House of Flowers shuddered again, and then took off up the fairy hill at a bouncing canter.

Rinaldo fell to the floor. Ygraine and Queenie clung to the tangled vine walls. Cornwall yowled once and then ducked under Orlando's feet, finding some hiding place.

The magic of the House of Flowers welcomed Rinaldo's proximity, his touch, but it shook off any attempt at control. Orlando had the wheel. He had always been able to slip past Rinaldo's guard, climbing into his magic as if it was his own. *Rinaldo had always let him.*

"Orlando, you're scaring us," said Ygraine, trying to sound brave. "Won't you tell us what your plan is?"

Orlando batted his eyes at her. "Darling Duchess, I'm doing what I've always done. What the Miraculous and Extraordinary Device Brothers have always done. We serve women in power with our magic."

"That's not true," Rinaldo sputtered, while realising that in fact, that was a good description of how they had spent the last decade or more. First the Empress of Britannia, then Lady Mortmain, and now... "You can't mean to serve the Queen of Faerie?"

"Why not?" said Orlando. "Hers is clearly the winning side. She has all the power. And with all this fresh air and clean living away from the smog and steam and steel of London, I'm thinking clearly for the first time since you built me to replace the brother you actually loved."

His words sank into Rinaldo like stones, hard and heavy. "It wasn't like that," he protested.

"Oh," said his brother, with a cruel glint to his mouth. "I think it was exactly like that. Hang on, my dears, the landing is going to be rough!"

"Here comes my gate!" declared the Faerie Queen.

An enormous house built from twigs and foliage and flowers surged into view, propelled on two massive root legs. The fairies screamed, laughed and scattered to make way as the house collapsed on to the ground near the mass of brambles imprisoning the wounded Lord Perrault.

The door blew open from the inside. The fairies nudged each other, leaning in to see what might emerge.

First: a yellow cat, which skidded down the front step as if something was after it and powered across the courtyard to climb up the trunk of a mango tree.

Him, Flavia reminded herself. *That's a Duke.*

Second: Princess Ygraine, her dark hair finally winning the battle against the last of her hairpins. It fell in a wild snarl over both shoulders, and down her back. Her blue dress was torn, and the princess limped a little, aided out of the house by Miss Queenie Gloucester. Queenie, of course, was stoic as ever despite being thoroughly rumpled.

The two of them made their way around the edge of the crowd of curious fairies.

Flavia gave up all appearance of impartiality and ran to them, reaching out. Queenie ducked away from a hug, but Ygraine received it instead, and was probably the greater in need. Flavia clung to her for a moment, breathing in her warmth. The two of them found each other's hands and hung on tightly.

"What a marvellous audience!" declared the voice of a showman, as Orlando Device strolled out of the odd house with his brother trailing reluctantly behind.

The Water of Hate kicked in, reminding Flavia how much she detested Orlando's very being. It felt more muted than before, and she found herself distracted by the utterly wrecked expression on the face of Rinaldo Device.

What could have happened between those two?

"My engineers!" declared Gloriana, getting to her feet. "My beautiful boys. I knew you would not let me down."

Rinaldo looked sickened. Orlando curled his arm into that of his brother's and walked them forward, grinning all over his horrid, beautiful face. "Ladies and gentlemen, fairies and... whatever this gnarled fellow is, gnome you say? Fascinating. We have some pixies in the house tonight, give it up for the pixies!" He led a rather bemused round of applause. "I present to you all: The House of Flowers. As with all of the best and most ingenious creations of the Extraordinary and Miraculous Device Brothers, it is infused with both our magics and a hefty dose of metallurmagic. Once you have fed it with the necessary blood — oh, I see you prepared some earlier — you will have your gateway back to Britannia, and your new lives!"

Now the fairies responded with more genuine gratitude and glee, applauding him wildly. Those who were already prepared with their 'mortal' clothes could barely be held back.

Orlando put in quite the performance, clasping a hand to his bosom and professing modesty. "I couldn't have done it without my beloved brother Rinaldo... but he would never have done it without me, so he needn't take any of the acclaim!"

He pushed Rinaldo away from him — more than a push, it must have been infused with magic, for his brother staggered away as if propelled by a great wind, collapsing at Flavia's feet.

As Orlando continued with some grandiose speech, parading himself before Gloriana, Rinaldo got up and started some kind of furious whispered conversation with Ygraine. They couldn't get very far away because Ygraine and Flavia were still holding hands.

Flavia heard Ygraine whisper: "Not my fault... Water of Truth," and a moment later, "Can't believe you never told him yourself!"

"I never told him," Rinaldo said in a furious undertone. "Because not knowing kept him *human*. Now look at him. He's about as real as they are, no wonder he's taking her side."

Flavia snorted.

Rinaldo blinked at her. "Excuse me?"

"Not real," she scoffed at him. "Of course he's real."

"Have you not been paying attention, Miss

Wednesday?" said Ygraine. "Orlando Device is an automaton. His brother made him out of scrap metal filings and sparks to take the place of a boy who died, like replacing every panel of a gown until there's nothing left of the original."

"What rot," said Flavia, dismissing them both. "What does it matter if he came from teaspoons and magic instead of flesh? I'm made mostly of dandelion seeds and fairy magic and — lawn clippings." She waved her replacement arm at them both, to prove her point. "You don't hear me having a crisis about it."

Rinaldo stared at her blankly.

Admittedly, it was hard to summon much sympathy for Orlando Device in his current mode as ringmaster of a particularly disturbing circus. He summoned his magics to hurl Perrault in his bramble cage at the House of Flowers, trapping the unconscious man on the roof with arms and legs splayed wildly out.

It was around that moment that Queenie Gloucester spotted her brother in the crowd. "Dash."

"Stop her," yelped Flavia, not quite close enough to collar the girl. Rinaldo grasped for her, but Queenie applied an elbow and kept running to what she thought was her brother.

Quicksilver's hand lashed up, grasping Queenie's face to stop her coming too near. "Will we need this one?" she asked in Dash's voice.

Orlando turned, and his own cruel expression faltered a little. "Let's not waste useful blood," he said.

"You never know when you'll need to take another journey."

The fairies laughed.

Flavia hated them in that moment, Orlando most of all. But she had seen that flicker. "He has a plan," she whispered reluctantly. "I think we're going to have to trust him."

"Oh dear," said Ygraine. "Are things as bad as all that?"

Rinaldo jerked as if he had been shot, and stared at the House of Flowers in horror. "It's starting. It's using my magic... I can't stop it."

The flowers of the house burst into bloom.

"Don't go too far, professor," called out Orlando Device with that nasty showman's smile of his. "We'll need someone to stoke the boiler."

Flavia found herself moving before she had even made a decision. She probably made a more comical figure than she might like, green-skinned in her ragged brown dress and no corset underneath. The fairies of her mother's court laughed at her as she marched forward. Flavia ignored her mother, marching up to the gentleman who still made her stomach churn with hatred. She turned her governess voice up to its most strident, channelling her former gym mistress from her clenched gut to her accusing finger, poking him directly in the chest.

"Orlando Device, what do you think you are doing?"

Orlando gave her a besotted smile. Oh, she had forgotten that complication. He was as in love with her as she was in hate with him. Why couldn't the fresh air of this land have cured him of *that*? "My dear Miss Wednesday. I'm about to pull off a miracle."

"You are aware that she's planning an invasion?" Flavia accused.

"Isn't that what you wanted?" Orlando replied, sweet as sugar. "You were all for the return of fairy magic to Britannia. It was the sacrifice you couldn't stomach. The children. Thanks to your friend Quicksilver, we found a solution." He blew a kiss to Quicksilver, and gestured dramatically at the Honourable Perrault, prostrate on the roof of the House of Flowers. "It's been a team effort. I'm terribly proud of us all."

"Why would you betray your own people for the fairies?" Flavia demanded.

Orlando's facade slipped away. For the first time since he made his dramatic reappearance, he looked tired. "Britannia has shunned me my whole life. They think me foreign. Exotic. Oriental. Because I don't look like I was born within a stone's throw of Portsmouth. You think those are my people in that wretched, rain-drenched country? I'm not even made of the same materials."

Scrap metal filings and sparks.

Anger rose through Flavia, and she wasn't sure any more what was the Water of Hate and what was a natural response to the situation. "You can't just give in," she accused him.

"I'm not giving in," said Orlando. "I'm accepting my destiny. Magic over mortals. Queen Gloriana needed a gate that was not reliant on the old ways, not tied to the solstices or other limitations." He smirked. "I probably could have done it without a drop of Gloucester blood. But you can't deny the crowd their bread and circuses."

A wind whipped up around them, a wind of dust and petals. The excitement of the fairies around them was tangible.

"You need a gate!" Orlando Device declared the Queen of Faerie. "Let there be gate."

The Honourable Perrault screamed, and his entire body sagged against the roof. Blood ran down the brambles and vines that wrapped around him, dripping into the House of Flowers.

The door at the front peeled back, pulling away the whole front face of the house like opening a tin of sardines.

The fairies chittered and sang.

Orlando smiled across at Flavia. "Forgive me," he said. "But you're a little too wholesome. I think a governess will be a liability where we're going. We plan to behave very badly." He gave the Queen a brief glance, as if asking a question.

"Her use to me ended on All Hallows Eve," said Flavia's mother with a shrug. "Leave her behind."

"As you wish," said Orlando, and bowed one last time.

Flavia was going to have Orlando Device dissected. She would hand him over to the alchemists and let them find new ways to break him down into liquids.

"I am ready to feed on mortal pain again!" declared the Queen to her fairies. "What about the rest of you? Ready to rend their land raw?"

The fairy hordes screeched with delight. The air was full of them, all buzzing wings and grasping fingers. They flooded the sky in an instant, blocking out the pale sun as they poured down and around their Queen, and into the House of Flowers. A gate to another world.

There was wind and magic everywhere. It tasted green and lush and so sweet that it seared the inside of her mouth. Flavia could not move her feet. She stared across to Princess Ygraine, who was likewise standing still as everything else went wild around them.

Tallow-wisp and Nightwhisper, Borage and Mead-owsweet, Dandelion and Sweet-pease, all vanished inside the House of Flowers.

Quicksilver, still in the body of Dashmond Gloucester, went after them, dragging Queenie along. There was nothing Flavia could do to prevent it. Magic washed over them all.

The yellow cat was dragged by unseen hands down from the mango tree and across the ground. Yowling and spitting sparks, he tumbled and shook and transformed into the body of a fair-haired man in bright scarlet military uniform, wide-eyed in shock.

Ygraine opened her mouth to call to him, but the Duke of Cornwall and Land's End was whisked into the house by an invisible force.

Rinaldo went next, flung about like a paper doll on a bonfire, his crumpled body sucked into the house he had brought to life with his own magic.

Finally, Orlando Device extended a hand to the Queen of Faerie. They promenaded together into the House of Flowers which folded up itself, smaller and smaller, until there was nothing left but a small flutter of petals on the breeze.

Flavia and Ygraine were left behind.

Ygraine
Duchess of Cornwall and Land's End

On the morning of my wedding, I awoke with a headache. I was dressed in my elaborate green wedding gown, and stood with my bridesmaids for what felt like hours, waiting for the carriage to take us from Buckingham Palace to Westminster Cathedral.

For some reason my mother had chosen yellow flowers for my bouquet, though I'd always hated them. It didn't matter. I suppose it was to match the silly yellow braid all over my bridegroom's uniform.

I walked down the aisle on the arm of the Queen of Britannia and Empress of India and half the world. Our procession included a selection of young ladies from good families as my bridesmaids, and also four exquisite maids of honour made from clockwork and French lace, who trilled harp music and dove cries from within their perfect torsos.

I married the Duke of Cornwall and Land's End.

We returned to the palace, and I waved to the crowd from the East Balcony with my new husband at my side.

There was wine at the wedding breakfast, but I didn't drink any. I kept thinking about my dream, how thirsty I had been. Today, I only drank lemon water and one cup of tea.

We had a fine five-tier cake covered in sugar almonds and green fondant leaves. More yellow flowers, not only of fondant, but also real flowers decorating the tables.

They would wilt, soon enough: the ballroom in Buckingham Palace was like a roasting pit once all the candles were alight.

Orkney attended the whole affair, escorting Evanna's motherless children with him: nine-year-old Gawain, the Prince of Wales and heir to Mama's Empire. His brothers Agravaine, Gaheris and Gareth, surrounded by nannies and nursemaids.

Arwenna was here, on the arm of her Marquess, utterly delighted with life as long as he was close enough to dote upon. The two of them had never had children, and no one seemed to mind. She had survived ten years of marriage, after all, which made her a rare flower in our family.

The automated maids-of-honour led the dancing with meticulous expertise. I danced in the arms of my new husband. It was all going rather well.

~

"You don't have to," Archie murmured, as the philtre was brought towards us on a silver salver. There were two matching goblets: one gold and one silver, with the same pretty details.

I noticed that he looked rather pale. "You don't have to either," I assured him.

"Oh," he said, looking rather grim. "I'm afraid I do. It won't work, otherwise."

For some reason, when he said it, he looked across the ballroom to where his valet, Mr Greenaway, was standing against a wall.

I had not seen Rinaldo or Orlando for some time. I wondered idly where they were. They'd promised some kind of unforgettable entertainment.

The silver salver came closer, towards the lucky couple.

"There's always Love-me-not," I said lightly. "If we don't like it."

"We will like it," said my bridegroom. "That's rather the point. We'll both be terribly happy."

We reached for the cups, each of us.

The music started again: a Viennese quadrille, played a little too fast on some kind of high-pitched harp I'd never heard before. Only, it wasn't played at all. The sound emanated from the... oh, those *dratted* clockwork maids of honour. I knew I should have been keeping an eye on them.

The maids took to the centre of the ballroom, exquisitely graceful as they began the intricate dance, circling around each other. It was odd to see a quadrille performed only with women, but they were mesmerising.

I glanced around, to see that all of our guests had their attention caught by the strange, beautiful dance. Even Mama was satisfied, nodding with approval.

There they were: the perpetrators. Orlando and Rinaldo Device, hovering in the musician's gallery at the far end of the ballroom, partly concealed by the enormous pipes of the organ.

It was so very hot in here. Too many people, too many candles blazing from the candelabras overhead. So much red and gilt and opulence; you would think I would be immune to discomfort after all this time.

The crowd gasped.

Clockwork cats poured out from behind the organ, surrounding the clockwork dancers and weaving in and out of their ankles with alarming precision. I could not count how many there were: I gave up after a dozen.

"Is that supposed to happen?" asked Archie, leaning forward with a short laugh.

Looking back to the musician's gallery, I saw a horrified Rinaldo waving his hands at his smirking brother. "I think it's supposed to be a surprise... oh!"

One of the cats leaped away from the dance and ran directly at us. It leaped for Archie's lap, and managed to knock over the salver containing the gold and silver cups of love philtre.

(Clearly, it was no accident. Orlando Device always thinks he knows best.)

Philtre spilled across the parquet floor, pooling at my feet. I drew them up, not wanting to stain my shoes, and saw a face reflected in the spilled philtre. A strange face, like something out of a storybook: the bright eyes and long golden hair of a child, covered in a twisted mask made of branches.

The masked woman smiled, and the ballroom filled with screams. The maids of honour had gone rogue, seizing party guests and dragging them roughly into the dance. Gone was the exquisite grace — they moved erratically, as if their limbs were heavier than expected.

The clockwork cats spread out, hissing and snarling at the guests.

One of the maids lurched in my direction, the front of her bustier falling away to reveal a glass case full of whirring cogs and sparks. As I stared in horrified fascination, all the bronze workings seemed to melt, forming the shape of a branch like the jewellery tree that the Device brothers had made for me, years ago.

The branch uncurled, smashing the glass from within, and a blaze of glowing light came spooling out...

Archie grabbed me, turning me aside to shield me with his body, and then he was *gone*.

I stared at the new cat at my feet: bright yellow, like those awful flowers. He stared back at me, hissed, and spat a metal cog on the floor. Then he ran in a yellow streak across the ballroom.

I took off after him, but the maids of honour grabbed at me, tearing at the thickly ruched skirt of my wedding dress. It was that indignity, I believe, that finally tipped Mama from shock and horror into action.

As chaos and clockwork tore my wedding to shreds, I heard the voice of Queen Isolda rising above the din.

"Arrest the Royal Engineers!"

Of all the key figures of the Siege of Buckingham Palace, the most overlooked must be Archibalt Lyonesse, Duke of Cornwall and Land's End, son-in-law to Queen Isolda.

Little scholarship has been done on the life of Lyonesse. Unusually for an aristocrat of his era, there are almost no surviving letters or diaries in his hand, and barely a handful of documents written by his household staff.

Given the existence of more infamous and better-documented members of the Lyonesse family, such as the tragic Tristan, not to mention the circle of sisters who set London Society aflame in the 1920s, it might be considered justifiable that Archibalt Lyonesse has avoided attention. But a great many questions remain unanswered.

Where was Lyonesse between his wedding to Princess Ygraine in September 1878, and the beginning of the Siege itself in December of that year? No public appearances are recorded for him during this period, while the princess herself made several. Newspapers spread rumours about a rift between the couple, with at least one speculating that the bridegroom was dead, his body hidden by the Palace.

As Baldwin states in his new book, it would have seemed entirely credible that the young Duke might have fallen victim to the infamous Curse of the Pendragons — the surprise is that more newspapers did not run with the rumour.

Baldwin himself suggests a new theory, that Lyonesse's absence from the public eye was due to a secret kidnapping: the first shot in the war between mortals and fairies that would come to define the final act of the Isoldan Empire.

— Willoughby Linton, "*Pride of Lyonesse* by Cornelius Baldwin: a new approach to 1878," *Nova Zeeland Critical Review*, 2001

Chapter 11

In Which Two Travellers Are Left Behind

Faerie was silent.

It had never been a quiet land, even when a much younger Flavia stole her way in through her dreams. There had always been music or whispers or chitters... someone had always been laughing at her.

The Queen's illusions had all fallen away, leaving Flavia on the bare hillside, surrounded by grass and debris. No castle, pebbled paths, no mango trees.

When she could finally move her limbs, she dropped to sit on the ground and feel numb. Her whole life, she had thought if she could only reach this glorious land and immerse herself in her mother's world, if she could only reach out and touch Quicksilver's hand... she would never have to leave.

She could hear Ygraine moving around, poking around here and there.

"Oh, here's my cloak," said the princess idly, collecting the bundle of silk that, Flavia recalled, was wrapped around the remains of her own dress and corset. "That will be useful."

"For what?" Flavia said with a throat that felt terribly dry. She closed her eyes for a moment and when she opened them, Ygraine was standing in front of her, holding a cup.

It wasn't as prettily decorated as it had been on the queen's tea table. Just a plain silver cup. It was, however, full of water that looked clear and inviting.

"All the other cups have turned into acorn lids," said Ygraine, sounding almost apologetic.

"I'm not the least surprised." Flavia took a sip and felt a wave of refreshment surge over her. Her exhaustion faded, and more than that: when she nudged irritably at the core of hatred she had been holding for Orlando Device, she could not find it. She peered at the princess suspiciously. "Where did you get that water?"

"It comes with the cup, look!" Ygraine took the goblet and tipped out the remaining water, then handed it back to Flavia, full to the brim.

Flavia winced. Of course it was a magic cup. "I wish you'd told me that before I drank."

Still, she didn't feel bad. She felt strong and cleansed. As if the magic of this land could not touch her. "Did you drink from it?"

Ygraine looked worried. "Yes?"

"Can you still fly?"

The princess raised herself up on her toes and scrunched up her face. "Oh," she said in dismay. "No."

"I think that might be the Water of Undoing." A cup that produced endless philtre — and a most useful philtre at that. Queenie would... but Flavia could not show Queenie now.

"There goes one of my escape plans," said Ygraine in a huff, sitting down on the grass beside Flavia. "Not that it would have been very useful. I couldn't carry you over the lake."

Flavia blinked at her. "Over the..."

"I've seen it all from the air," Ygraine said, bubbling over with enthusiasm. "I think I can find the way, at least. We're in the middle of a lake, not an ocean. There's land, not far from here. The water between isn't even as wide as the Thames. If we built a boat, we could cross it."

Flavia gazed at the other woman. How was she not exhausted? How was she not defeated? "Can you build a boat?"

Ygraine scoffed. "I'm the daughter of Percival Pendragon, you just watch me build a boat." She followed up that extreme confidence with a question: "How are you at putting things together? With your magic, that is. You do have magic, don't you? We might be rather sunk, otherwise."

Flavia breathed in. The Water of Undoing, if that was what she had drunk, had not affected her own innate magic. If it had, her right arm would be a pile of lawn clippings. She was surrounded by magic, in the air and in the land. Without all the fairies getting in the way, surely she could accomplish something with all this. "We can probably build a boat," she agreed. "That land you saw, it's the Forest of Arden. It's not your country. And the only way out of there..."

She paused and thought about it. Really thought about it.

Ygraine gazed at her impatiently, her eyes wide and luminous. Having all of the princess's attention directed right at Flavia was a heady thing. *She has a husband*, Flavia reminded herself. *Don't get any notions.*

"The Gate Sinister can only be opened on a Solstice, or an Equinox," she said after another moment. "The Winter Solstice was a few weeks away when we came through but..."

"We can't have been here more than a day or two," said Ygraine, and then her face crumpled as she thought about it. "I haven't slept. Have you slept?"

"Time is different here," said Flavia. "It could be weeks back in Britannia. It could be months." The thought of what her mother and the fairies could do to their world in months was horrifying... not that there was anything she could do to stop it.

"All right," said Ygraine, lifting her chin. "Even if it's been months... that just gets us closer to the next one. Yes? There are two solstices a year, two equinoxes. We'll get to one eventually."

"The gate needs the blood of a Gloucester to be opened," Flavia murmured, on the verge of admitting something else.

"Oh, well." Ygraine screwed up her nose a little. "Hate to say it, but there's a whole patch of it on the grass over there, from where they did what they did to that poor gentleman. It won't be fresh exactly, but we could carry a sample in a handkerchief." She rummaged in her sleeve and produced a square of embroidered linen that looked almost as delicate as a gown made of cobweb.

And that meant Flavia didn't have to admit: *I think I might have Gloucester blood of my own in my veins.* Not out loud, in any case.

She got to her feet, and held out a hand to Ygraine, who took it with a warm, dizzying smile.

"You really think we can do this," said Flavia, not quite believing it. "We can travel across this land on our own, cross the Lake of All Worlds and the Forest of Arden, open the Gate Sinister and *go home.*"

Ygraine flung herself at Flavia, embracing her tightly. She smelled of crushed mint and violets. "Of course we can!" Ygraine pulled back for a moment and pressed a kiss with careful determination to Flavia's cheek. Then she twisted away, hurrying with enthusiasm to collect blood-stained grass into her handkerchief. "I am not going to be the princess who disappeared into the Land of Faerie and never came home!" she called behind her. "That's not my story."

Flavia watched the princess go, feeling the blazing imprint of lips on her cheek, as if the kiss was still happening.

Home, she thought when she could finally assemble her thoughts into something sensible. *I thought of Britannia, and I said 'home.'*

End

Siege Miraculous

Thank you so much for reading the third book in the Sparks & Philtres series! Flavia, Ygraine, Orlando, Rinaldo, Queenie, Dash, Cornwall, the Queen of the Fairies and the Empress of Britannia will all return one last time in the final volume of this series:

SIEGE MIRACULOUS
(SPARKS & PHILTRES #4)

One Last Epic Journey Through the Forest of Arden, Sparks Bringing Metal To Life, Love Philtres Conquered, Family Rifts Repaired, Fairies Running Amok on Britannian Soil, and the entirely newsworthy Siege of Buckingham Palace.

About the Author

Tansy Rayner Roberts is an award-winning Australian science fiction and fantasy author who enjoys quilting and chateau-themed TV shows. She lives with her family in Tasmania and has the complete opposite of botanical magic.

- Listen to Tansy on Sheep Might Fly, a podcast where she reads aloud her stories as audio serials.
- Read Tansy's stories before anyone else when you pledge to her Patreon.
- What tea is Tansy drinking? Find out when you subscribe to her excellent newsletter.

facebook.com/TansyRRoberts

instagram.com/tansyrr

patreon.com/tansyrr

bookbub.com/authors/tansy-rayner-roberts

amazon.com/stores/Tansy-Rayner-Roberts/author/B00JLK9Y0C